projects

featuring Sirdar, Rowan, and Jaeger yarns

Reader's Digest

contents

SIMPLE TO KNIT

Starting with the bag you can knit from the yarn in your kit, here are some simple projects to try your hand at.

In *The Complete Knitting Set* you will find DK yarn, a pair of knitting needles, a cable needle, a blunt-ended yarn needle, a stitch holder, yarn bobbins, plus cotton lining fabric, a sewing needle, and thread. Use these to make project 1, Knitted bag.

TERRIFIC TEXTURES

One of the delights of knitting is creating fabric with texture. Here are some of the best.

COLORFUL COLLECTION

Put color into your world and that of your friends and family with these wonderful bright designs.

techniques ▶

You will find boxes like this throughout this book. They refer to the relevant sections in your techniques book.

simple to knit

Simply the best—this collection of projects, in a variety of exciting yarns, has something for everyone. Create a trendy bag—perfect for new knitters. Dress a baby in a sporty hooded top. Embroider a cute figure on the back of a child's cardigan. Send him sailing in a casual sweater knitted in a denim-style yarn. Plus a classic jacket that you can knit in no time at all.

SKILL 1

FOR THE BEGINNER

USE THE EQUIPMENT
AND YARN IN YOUR
KIT TO MAKE A
HANDY LITTLE BAG
FOR ALL THOSE
ODDS AND ENDS.
CATCH UP ON YOUR
TECHNIQUES AND ADD
INTERESTING CABLES,
OR SIMPLY LEAVE THE
BAG PLAIN AND
DECORATE IT WITH
EYE-CATCHING
BUTTONS.

Knitted bag

knitted bag

For this first project, the instructions are written in two ways—without abbreviations for beginners and in the conventional, abbreviated form of knitting patterns for those who prefer it.

ABBREVIATIONS

C7B = Cable 7 back: Slip next 4 sts onto cable needle and hold at back, k3 then k 4 sts from cable needle; **k** = knit; **p** = purl; **rep** = repeat; **RS** = right side; **s-st** = seed stitch; **st(s)** = stitch(es); **St st** = stockinette stitch; **WS** = wrong side.

pattern notes

The instructions for this cable bag are given twice. On the right are the row-by-row instructions, written out in full without abbreviations, and an abbreviated version is on page 9. Choose which set of instructions to follow, according to your level of skill. If you prefer to work from a chart, you will find one for the cable bag on page 9.

CABLE BAG (IN FULL)
FRONT

Using size 6 (4mm) needles, cast on 27 stitches.

1st Row: (right side) Knit 1, *purl 1, knit 1, repeat from * to end of row. Repeat this row (to form seed stitch) 3 times more.
5th Row: Knit 1, purl 1, knit 1, purl 21, knit 1, purl 1, knit 1.
6th Row: Knit 1, purl 1, knit 23, purl 1, knit 1.**
Repeat rows 5 and 6 once more.
The first 3 stitches and the last 3 stitches of rows 9–36 are worked knit 1, purl 1,

techniques ▶

For casting on   p. 10

For seed stitch   p. 18

For stockinette stitch p. 17

The shaped cable needle in your kit is ideal if you are new to working cables. The stitches on the cable needle "sit" securely in the shaped section until you need them again.

knit 1 and referred to as "seed stitch 3."

9th Row: Seed stitch 3, purl 10, knit 1, purl 10, seed stitch 3.

10th Row: Seed stitch 3, knit 10, purl 1, knit 10, seed stitch 3.

11th Row: Seed stitch 3, purl 9, knit 3, purl 9, seed stitch 3.

12th Row: Seed stitch 3, knit 9, purl 3, knit 9, seed stitch 3.

13th Row: Seed stitch 3, purl 8, knit 5, purl 8, seed stitch 3.

14th Row: Seed stitch 3, knit 8, purl 5, knit 8, seed stitch 3.

15th Row: Seed stitch 3, purl 7, knit 7, purl 7, seed stitch 3.

16th Row: Seed stitch 3, knit 7, purl 7, knit 7, seed stitch 3.

Repeat rows 15 and 16 twice more.

21st Row: Seed stitch 3, purl 7, slip next 4 stitches onto a cable needle and hold at back, knit 3, then knit 4 stitches from cable needle, purl 7, seed stitch 3.

22nd, 24th, and 26th Rows: As 16th row.

23rd and 25th Rows: As 15th row.

27th Row: As 13th row.

28th Row: As 14th row.

29th Row: As 11th row.

30th Row: As 12th row.

31st Row: As 9th row.

32nd Row: As 10th row.

33rd and 35th Rows: As 5th row.

34th and 36th Rows: As 6th row.

***37th Row:** As first row.

Repeat last row 7 times more. Bind off.

BACK

Work as given for front, but omit cable motif and work entirely in reverse stockinette stitch with seed-stitch borders.

TO FINISH

Make 2 handles by cutting two 39in (100cm) lengths of yarn for each one.

Double the strands and knot together at the free ends to form a ring. Loop the ring over a door handle, insert a pencil at the knot end and twist until tight. Bring both ends together into a twisted cord and secure. Using knitting yarn, join the front and back of the bag by oversewing the sides and base on the right side. Turn the top border in half to the wrong side and stitch down. Stitch the handles to the bound-off edge of the border. Fold the lining fabric in half lengthways, place the bag base on the fold and draw around this. Cut out, adding ¾in (2cm) turnings to the sides. Seam the sides and turn down 1in (2.5cm) at the top edge to the wrong side. Insert the lining in the bag and stitch down around the top edge.

techniques
For cables   p. 28
For binding off   p. 15

Cable Bag (abbreviated)

Front

Using size 6 (4mm) needles, cast on 27 sts.

1st Row: (RS) K1, *p1, k1, rep from * to end.

Rep last row (for s-st) 3 times more.

5th Row: K1, p1, k1, p21, k1, p1, k1.

6th Row: K1, p1, k23, p1, k1.**

Rep rows 5 and 6 once more.

Note: The first 3 sts and the last 3 sts of rows 9–36 are worked k1, p1, k1 to form s-st borders.

9th Row: S-st3, p10, k1, p10, s-st3.

10th Row: S-st3, k10, p1, k10, s-st3.

11th Row: S-st3, p9, k3, p9, s-st3.

12th Row: S-st3, k9, p3, k9, s-st3.

13th Row: S-st3, p8, k5, p8, s-st3.

14th Row: S-st3, k8, p5, k8, s-st3.

15th Row: S-st3, p7, k7, p7, s-st3.

16th Row: S-st3, k7, p7, k7, s-st3.

Rep rows 15 and 16 twice more.

21st Row: S-st3, p7, C7B, p7, s-st3.

22nd, 24th, and 26th Rows: As 16th row.

23rd and 25th Rows: As 15th row.

27th Row: As 13th row.

keep track

A row counter helps you to record where you are in a pattern so that if you have to put your knitting down, you will know exactly which row to work when you return to it.

Chart for Cable Design

Key

☐ = k on RS rows, p on WS rows

▪ = p on RS rows, k on WS rows

⧅⧄⧅⧄ = C7B (see abbreviations on page 7)

28th Row: As 14th row.

29th Row: As 11th row.

30th Row: As 12th row.

31st Row: As 9th row.

32nd Row: As 10th row.

33rd and 35th Rows: As 5th row.

34th and 36th Rows: As 6th row.

***37th Row:** As first row.

Rep last row 7 times more. Bind off.

Back & To Finish

Work as given for version on page 8.

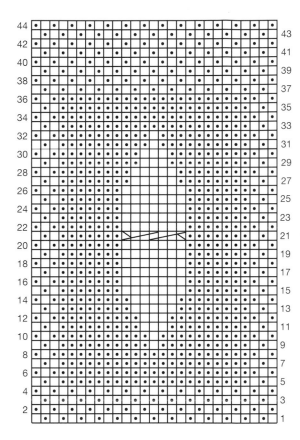

Design with Buttons

Work as given for Cable Bag to **.

Rep 5th and 6th rows 15 times more, then work as given for Cable Bag from *** to end, making Back and Front alike.

Sew buttons to front, then finish as given for Cable Bag.

toddler's v–neck cardigan

SKILL

2

PRACTICE
MAKES
PERFECT

THIS STOCKINETTE
STITCH CARDIGAN IS
QUICK AND EASY TO
MAKE IN A MEDIUM–
WEIGHT KNITTING
YARN. THE GARTER–
STITCH STRIPE
ADDS A COLORFUL
TOUCH AND THE
CUTE BACK VIEW,
EMBROIDERED ON
AFTERWARD, IS
SUCH FUN.

toddler's v-neck cardigan   **project 2**

toddler's v-neck cardigan

If you are daunted by the thought of embroidering the design on the back of this cardigan, then leave it plain! Instead, you can work the garter-stitch stripe pattern on the back as well as the fronts and sleeves.

MEASUREMENTS

To fit chest		18	20	22
	in			
	cm	46	51	56
Actual Size	in	21	22¾	25¼
	cm	53	58	64
Length	in	10¼	11½	13½
	cm	26	29	34
Sleeve	in	6½	7	7½
	cm	17	18	19

Figures in brackets [ ] refer to larger sizes; where there is only one set of figures, it applies to all sizes.

YOU WILL NEED

Number of 50g (1¾oz) skeins Sirdar Country Style DK:

A (shade 412)	3	3	4
B (shade 442)	1	1	1
C (shade 489)	1	1	1
D (shade 419)	1	1	1

Small amounts of flesh-color and brown yarn for embroidery
Pair of size 6 (4mm) knitting needles
Pair of size 3 (3¼mm) knitting needles
4[4,5] buttons

GAUGE

22 sts and 28 rows to 4in (10cm) over St st on size 6 (4mm) needles or size required to give correct gauge.

ABBREVIATIONS

See page 95.

COLOR PATTERN

1st Row: Using A, knit.
2nd Row: Using A, purl.
Rep first and 2nd rows twice more.

7th and 8th Rows: Using B, knit.
Rep first–6th rows once more.
15th and 16th Rows: Using C, knit.
17th–22nd Rows: As first–6th rows.
23rd and 24th Rows: Using D, knit.
Rep first–24th rows to form Color Pat.

LEFT FRONT

Using smaller needles and A, cast on 24[28,30] sts.
1st Row: *K1, p1, rep from * to end.
Rep first row 10 times more to form 1x1 rib.
12th Row: Rib to end, inc 2[1,2] sts evenly across row. 26[29,32] sts.
Change to larger needles.
Work 36[40,52] rows in Color Pat.

SHAPE FRONT EDGE

Work 31[33,41] rows. Dec as follows:
1 st at end of next row (for Right Front, bind off at beg of row) and every foll 5th[4th,5th] rows. 19[20,23] sts.
Work 5[7,3] rows more without shaping.
Bind off in pat.

RIGHT FRONT

Work as given for Left Front, reversing shapings as indicated above.
.

BACK

Using smaller needles and A, cast on
57[63,69] sts.

Work in 1x1 rib for 11 rows.

12th Row: Rib to end, m1 in center of row.
58[64,70] sts.

Change to larger needles. Beg with a k
row, work in St st throughout until Back
matches Fronts to shoulders, ending with
a WS row.

Bind off.

SLEEVES

Using smaller needles and A, cast on
31[33,33] sts.

Work in 1x1 rib for 1¾ in (4cm), ending
with a RS row.

Next Row: Rib 1[2,2], m1, (rib 4, m1)
7 times, rib 2[3,3]. 39[41,41] sts.

Change to larger needles. Working in

Color Pat throughout, inc one st at each
end of 3rd and every foll 7th[5th,4th]
row to 49[55,61] sts, working inc sts
into pat.

Cont without shaping until sleeve
measures 6½[7,7½]in (17[18,19]cm),
ending with a WS row. Bind off in pat.

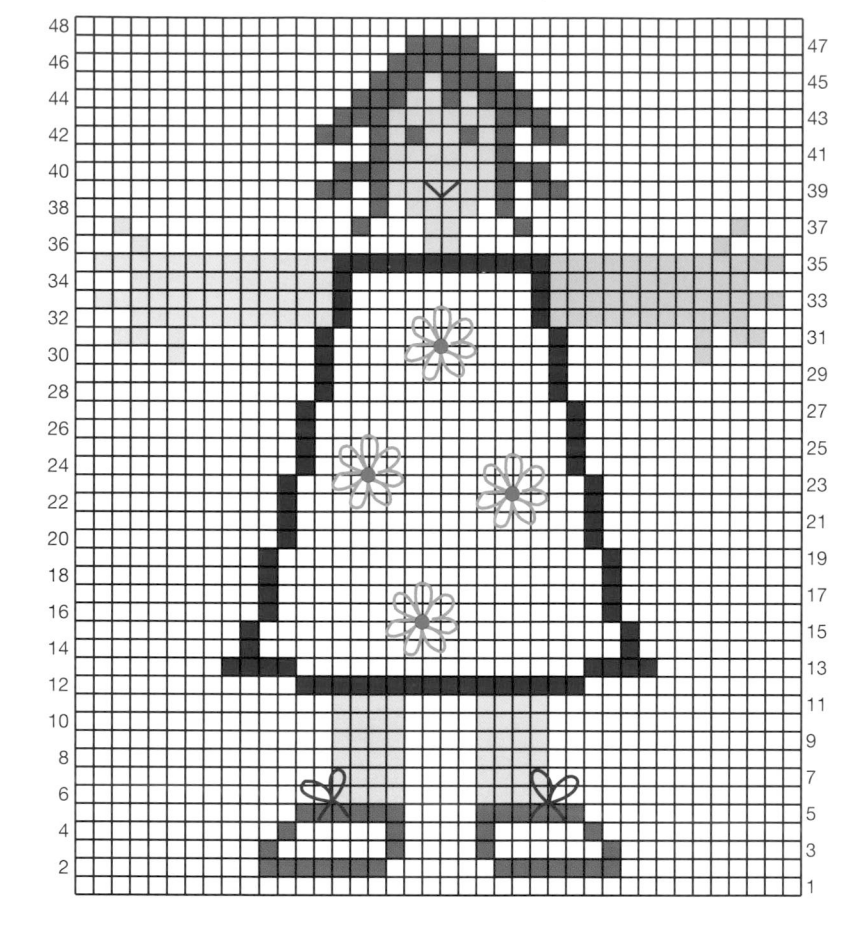

**CHART FOR
DUPLICATE
STITCH**

KEY

■ = B

▢ = flesh color

■ = brown

\ = straight stitch
in B

✗ = thread a short
length of B through
work and tie in a
small bow

✤ = lazy daisy stitch
petals in C with
French knot center
in D

techniques ▶

For duplicate stitch p. 38

For lazy daisy stitch p. 39

BORDER

Join shoulder seams.
Using smaller needles and A, and with RS facing, starting at bottom of right front, pick up and knit 10 sts evenly along rib, 31[34,42] sts evenly along straight edge, 28[32,36] sts evenly along shaped edge, 21[25,25] sts from back of neck, 28[32, 36] sts evenly along shaped edge, 31[34, 42] sts evenly along straight edge, and 10 sts evenly along rib. 159[177,201] sts. Work 3 rows in 1x1 rib.

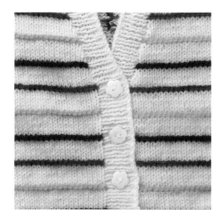

For a Boy

Next Row: Rib 3, bind off 2 sts, (rib 8[9,8], bind off 2 sts) 3[3,4] times, rib to end.
Next Row: Rib to last 30[33,39] sts, cast on 2 sts, (rib 9[10,9], cast on 2 sts) 3[3,4] times, rib 3.

For a Girl

Next Row: Rib to last 38[41,49] sts, bind off 2 sts, (rib 8[9,8], bind off 2 sts, 3[3,4] times, rib 2.
Next Row: Rib 3, cast on 2 sts, (rib 9[10, 9], cast on 2 sts) 3[3,4] times, rib to end.

For Girl and Boy

Work 3 more rows in rib. Bind off in rib.

---

be button wise

Take the garment with you when buying buttons to double-check for size and color. On a plain garment, you might prefer to select a novelty button from the wide range available for children.

TO FINISH

Press according to directions on yarn label. Following the chart on previous page, work the girl's figure in duplicate stitch in the center of the back. When the duplicate stitch is complete, embroider straight stitches for the girl's mouth and lazy daisy stitch flowers, with French knot centers, on her dress. Decorate the shoes with bows.

Fold sleeves in half lengthwise, then placing folds at shoulder seams, sew sleeves in position. Join side and sleeve seams. Sew buttons on appropriate front.

MEASUREMENTS

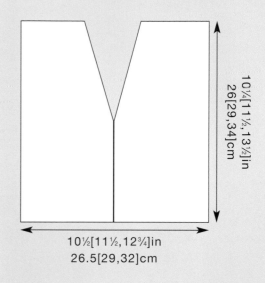

10¼[11½,13½]in
26[29,34]cm

10½[11½,12¾]in
26.5[29,32]cm

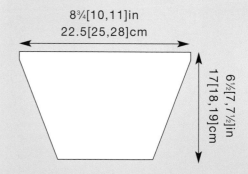

8¾[10,11]in
22.5[25,28]cm

6½[7,7½]in
17[18,19]cm

woman's chunky jacket

SKILL

1

FOR THE
BEGINNER

WITH ITS LONGER
LENGTH AND RAGLAN
SLEEVES, THIS SIMPLE
STOCKINETTE STITCH
JACKET, IN A SOFT,
DENIM-STYLE TWEEDY
YARN, IS SURE TO BE
A WINNER. YOU CAN
DRESS IT UP FOR
SHOPPING IN TOWN
OR TEAM IT WITH
CASUAL WEAR FOR A
DAY IN THE
COUNTRY.

woman's chunky jacket   **project 3**

woman's chunky jacket

If you want an easy knit in a timeless style, this jacket is perfect. The plain stockinette stitch fabric is bordered with deep, ribbed bands, while the collar and pockets are good-looking features that are practical as well.

MEASUREMENTS

To fit bust		32	34	36	38	40
	in	32	34	36	38	40
	cm	81	86	91	97	102
Actual Size	in	40	42	43¾	45¼	47¼
	cm	102	107	111	115	120
Length	in	32	32¼	33	33	33
	cm	81	82	84	84	84
Sleeve	in	16	17	17	17	17
	cm	41	43	43	43	43

Figures in brackets [ ] refer to larger sizes; where there is only one set of figures, it applies to all sizes.

YOU WILL NEED

Number of 100g (3½oz) skeins Sirdar Denim Ultra (shade 614):

		9	10	10	11	11

Pair of size 15 (10mm) knitting needles
Pair of size 11 (8mm) knitting needles
5 buttons

GAUGE

9 sts and 12 rows to 4in (10cm) over St st on size 15 (10mm) needles or the size required to give the correct gauge.

ABBREVIATIONS

See page 95.

BACK

Using larger needles, cast on 46[46,50, 50,54] sts.

1st Row: (RS) K2, *p2, k2, rep from * to end.
2nd Row: *P2, k2, rep from * to last 2 sts, p2.
These 2 rows will now be referred to as 2x2 rib. Work in 2x2 rib for 3in (8cm), ending with a RS row.
Next Row: Rib to end, inc 2 sts evenly across row for 2nd and 4th sizes only. 46[48,50,52,54] sts.
Proceed as follows:
1st Row: Knit.
2nd Row: Purl.
These 2 rows will be referred to as St st (stockinette stitch). Working in St st throughout, cont until back measures 21¾[21¾,21¾,21½,21¼]in (55[55,55, 54,54]cm), ending with a WS row.

SHAPE RAGLAN ARMHOLES

Bind off 3[3,3,3,4] sts at beg of next 2 rows. 40[42,44,46,46] sts.
Proceed as follows:
1st Row: K1, p1, sl1-k1-psso, knit to last 4 sts, k2tog, p1, k1.
2nd Row: P2, p2tog, purl to last 4 sts, p2tog tbl, p2. 36[38,40,42,42] sts.
First and 2nd rows set raglan shapings. Work 4[4,4,2,2] rows, dec one st at each end as before in every row. 28[30,32,38, 38] sts.

techniques ▶

For buttonholes   p. 43

Proceed as follows:
1st Row: K1, p1, sl1-k1-psso, knit to last 4 sts, k2tog, p1, k1. 26[28,30,36,36] sts.
2nd Row: Purl.
First and 2nd rows set raglan shapings.
Work 14[16,18,22,22] rows, dec one st at each end as before in next and every foll alt row.
Bind off rem 12[12,12,14,14] sts.

POCKET LININGS (MAKE 2)

Using larger needles, cast on 16 sts.
Work in St st for 6in (15cm), ending with a WS row.
Leave these 16 sts on a stitch holder.

LEFT FRONT

Using larger needles, cast on 19[23,23, 23,27] sts.

1st Row: (RS) K2, *p2, k2, rep from * to last st, p1.
2nd Row: K1, *p2, k2, rep from * to last 2 sts, p2.
First and 2nd rows set 2x2 rib.
Work in rib for 3in (8cm), ending with a RS row.
Next Row: Rib to end, inc 2[0,0,1,0] sts evenly across row or dec 0[1,0,0,2] sts evenly across row. 21[22,23,24,25] sts.
Working in St st throughout, cont until left front measures 11in (28cm), ending with a WS row.

practical pockets

Inset pockets are the neatest pocket solution since the seams are on the wrong side of the work and invisible. The linings are worked first, then knitted into the main fabric behind the pocket opening.

PLACE POCKET

Next Row: K3[4,5,5,6], slip next 16 sts onto a stitch holder, knit across 16 sts left on stitch holder for one pocket lining, k2[2,2,3,3]. 21[22,23,24,25] sts.
Next Row: Purl.
Cont until left front measures 21¾[21¾, 21¾,21½,21¼]in (55[55,55,54,54]cm), ending with a WS row.

SHAPE RAGLAN ARMHOLE

Next Row: Bind off 3[3,3,3,4] sts, knit to end. 18[19,20,21,21] sts.
Next Row: Purl.
Proceed as follows:
1st Row: K1, p1, sl1-k1-psso, knit to end.
2nd Row: Purl to last 4 sts, p2tog tbl, p2. 16[17,18,19,19] sts.
First and 2nd rows set raglan shapings.
Work 4[4,4,2,2] rows, dec one st at raglan edge as before in every row. 12[13,14, 17,17] sts. Proceed as follows:
1st Row: K1, p1, sl1-k1-psso, knit to end. 11[12,13,16,16] sts.
2nd Row: Purl.
First and 2nd rows set raglan shapings.
Work 11[13,15,19,19] rows, dec one st at raglan edge as before in next and every foll alt row. 5[5,5,6,6] sts.

SHAPE NECK

Next Row: Bind off 1[1,1,2,2] sts, p3. 4 sts.
Next Row: K1, sl1-k2tog-psso. 2 sts.
Next Row: P2tog. Fasten off.

RIGHT FRONT

Using larger needles, cast on 19[23,23, 23,27] sts.
1st Row: (RS) P1, k2, *p2, k2, rep from * to end.

2nd Row: *P2, k2, rep from * to last 3 sts, p2, k1.

First and 2nd rows set rib. Work in rib for 3in (8cm), ending with a RS row.

Next Row: Rib to end, inc 2[0,0,1,0] sts evenly across row or dec 0[1,0,0,2] sts evenly across row. 21[22,23,24,25] sts. Working in St st throughout, cont until right front measures 11in (28cm), ending with a WS row.

PLACE POCKET

Next Row: K2[2,2,3,3], slip next 16 sts onto a stitch holder, knit across 16 sts left on stitch holder for other pocket lining, k3[4,5,5,6].

Next Row: Purl.

Cont until right front measures 21¾[21¾, 21¾,21¼,21¼]in (55[55,55,54,54]cm), ending with a RS row.

raglan shaping

The decreased stitches at either side of a raglan armhole form a neat border, sloping the same way as the edge. For paired decreases, see the techniques book, page 23.

SHAPE RAGLAN ARMHOLE

Next Row: Bind off 3[3,3,3,4] sts, purl to end. 18[19,20,21,21] sts.

1st Row: Knit to last 4 sts, k2tog, p1, k1.

2nd Row: P2, p2tog, purl to end. 16[17,18,19,19] sts.

First and 2nd rows set raglan shapings. Work 4[4,4,2,2] rows, dec 1 st at raglan edge as before in every row. 12[13,14,17, 17] sts. Proceed as follows:

1st Row: Knit to last 4 sts, k2tog, p1, k1. 11[12,13,16,16] sts.

2nd Row: Purl.

First and 2nd rows set raglan shapings. Work 10[12,14,18,18] rows, dec one st at raglan edge as before in next and every foll alt row. 6[6,6,7,7] sts.

SHAPE NECK

Next Row: Bind off 1[1,1,2,2] sts, k2tog, p1, k1. 4 sts.

Next Row: Purl.

Next Row: K3tog, k1. 2 sts.

Next Row: P2tog. Fasten off.

SLEEVES

Using smaller needles, cast on 22[22,22,26,26] sts. Work in 2x2 rib for 3in (8cm), ending with a WS row. Change to larger needles. Work in St st throughout, inc 1 st at each end of 3rd and every foll 4th row to 36[34,40, 32,38] sts.

For first, 2nd, 4th, and 5th sizes only

Inc one st at each end of every foll 6th row to 38[38,40,42] sts.

For all 5 sizes

Cont without shaping until sleeve measures 16[17,17,17,17]in (41[43,43, 43,43]cm), ending with a WS row.

SHAPE RAGLAN TOP

Bind off 3[3,3,3,4] sts at beg of next 2 rows. 32[32,34,34,34] sts.
Proceed as follows:

For first size only
1st Row: Sl1-k1-psso, knit to last 2 sts, k2tog.
2nd Row: P2tog, purl to last 2 sts, p2tog tbl. 28 sts.

For 4th and 5th sizes only
1st Row: Sl1-k1-psso, knit to last 2 sts, k2tog. [32,32] sts.
2nd Row: Purl.
3rd Row: Knit.
4th Row: Purl.

For all 5 sizes
1st Row: Sl1-k1-psso, knit to last 2 sts, k2tog. 26[30,32,30,30] sts.
2nd Row: Purl.
First and 2nd rows set raglan shapings. Work 18[22,24,22,22] rows, dec one st at each end as before in next and every foll alt row. 8 sts. Bind off rem 8 sts.

neat buttons

Buttons with a flat back and sewing holes, rather than a protruding shank, sit neatly on a stretchy knitted fabric.

MEASUREMENTS

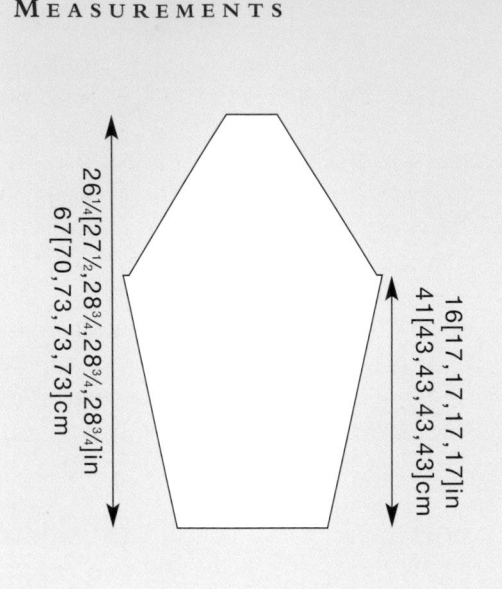

26¼[27½,28¾,28¾,28¾]in 67[70,73,73,73]cm

16[17,17,17,17]in 41[43,43,43,43]cm

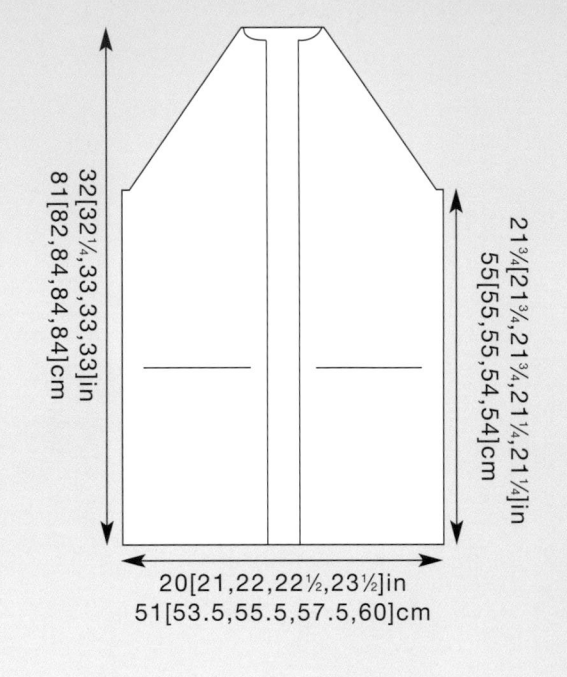

32[32¼,33,33,33]in 81[82,84,84,84]cm

21¾[21¾,21¾,21¼,21¼]in 55[55,55,54,54]cm

20[21,22,22½,23½]in 51[53.5,55.5,57.5,60]cm

RIGHT FRONT BORDER

Using smaller needles and with RS facing, pick up and knit 8 sts evenly along rib and 74[74,74,78,78] sts evenly along front edge. 82[82,82,86,86] sts.
Starting with 2nd row of 2x2 rib, work 3 rows.
Next Row: Rib 25[25,25,29,29], bind off 2 sts, (rib 10, bind off 2 sts) 4 times, rib 2.
Next Row: Rib 3, cast on 2 sts, (rib 11, cast on 2 sts) 4 times, rib 25[25,25,29,29].

Work 3 rows more in 2x2 rib.
Bind off in rib.

LEFT FRONT BORDER

Work to match Right Front Border, omitting buttonholes.

COLLAR

Join raglan seams.

Using smaller needles and with RS facing, start at center of right front border and pick up and knit 8[8,8,9,9] sts evenly along right side of neck, 8 sts from top of sleeve, 12[12,12,14,14] sts from back of neck, 8 sts from top of left sleeve, and 8[8,8,9,9] sts evenly along left side of neck, ending at center of left front border. 44[44,44,48,48] sts.

Next Row: P8[8,8,10,10], inc in next st purlwise, (p2, inc in next st purlwise) 9 times, p8[8,8,10,10]. 54[54,54,58,58] sts. Starting with 2nd row of 2x2 rib, work 4¼in (11cm), ending with a WS row.

Next Row: Rib 10, (inc in next st purlwise, p1, k2) 9[9,9,10,10] times, rib 8. 63[63,63,68,68] sts. Bind off in pat.

POCKET BORDERS

Using smaller needles and with RS facing, work across 16 sts left on stitch holder as follows:

Next Row: Cast on one st, work across 16 sts left on stitch holder for pocket border as follows—k4, (inc in next st, k5) twice, cast on one st. (Cast-on sts to be used for sewing pocket border to fronts.) 20 sts.

1st Row: K1, *p2, k2, rep from * to last 3 sts, p2, k1.

2nd Row: P1, k2, *p2, k2, rep from * to last st, p1.

Rep first and 2nd rows twice more. Bind off in rib.

TO FINISH

Join side and sleeve seams. Sew pocket linings and pocket borders in position. Sew on buttons. Pin out garment to the actual measurements given in the panel on page 18. Cover with damp cloths and allow to dry completely.

man's guernsey-style sweater

SKILL

1

FOR THE
BEGINNER

HE'LL LOVE THIS
FISHERMAN'S-STYLE
SWEATER THAT'S SO
PRACTICAL FOR
OUTDOOR WEAR.
KNITTED
IN A FASHIONABLE,
LIGHTWEIGHT
DENIM-STYLE YARN
AND WIDE RIB
PATTERN, IT HAS
TEXTURED-STITCH
PANELS ON THE YOKE.

man's guernsey-style sweater

Don't be put off by the textured panels on the yoke of this sweater—they are formed with combinations of basic knit and purl stitches. It's a simple version of a pattern common on fishermen's sweaters in days gone by.

MEASUREMENTS

To fit chest	in	38	40	42	44	46
	cm	97	102	107	112	117
Actual Size	in	42½	44½	46	48	50¾
	cm	108	113	117	122	129
Length	in	28¾	28¾	28¾	29½	30
	cm	73	73	73	75	76
Sleeve	in	18½	19	19¾	20	20½
	cm	47	48	51	52	53

Figures in brackets [ ] refer to larger sizes; where there is only one set of figures, it applies to all sizes.

YOU WILL NEED

Number of 50g (1¾oz) skeins Sirdar Denim Tweed DK (shade 502):

9	9	10	10	11

Pair of size 6 (4mm) knitting needles
Pair of size 3 (3¼mm) knitting needles

GAUGE

22 sts and 28 rows to 4in (10cm) over pattern, 22 sts and 32 rows to 4in (10cm) over yoke pattern on size 6 (4mm) needles or the size required to give the correct gauge.

ABBREVIATIONS

See page 95.

gauge testing

For a garment that fits correctly, it's important to check your gauge beforehand—see the techniques book, page 45. Once you achieve the correct gauge for the main pattern here, you will probably find that your gauge over the yoke pattern is correct as well.

BACK

Using smaller needles, cast on 119[125, 129,135,141] sts.
1st Row: K1, *p1, k1, rep from * to end.
2nd Row: *P1, k1, rep from * to last st, p1.

These 2 rows will now be referred to as 1x1 rib. Work in 1x1 rib for 1½[1½,1½,2, 2]in (4[4,4,5,5]cm), ending with a WS row. Change to larger needles and proceed as follows:
1st Row: K7[2,4,7,2], *p1, k7, rep from * to last 8[3,5,8,3] sts, p1, k7[2,4,7,2].
2nd Row: Purl.
First and 2nd rows set pat.
Cont in pat until back measures 15½in (39cm), ending with a WS row.

Proceed as follows:
1st and Every Alt Row: K7[2,4,7,2], *p1, k7, rep from * to last 8[3,5,8,3] sts, p1, k7[2,4,7,2].
2nd Row: K0[0,3,0,0], p0[3,2,0,3], *p1, k5, p2, rep from * to last 7[2,4,7,2] sts, p1[2,1,1,2], k5[0,3,5,0], p1[0,0,1,0].

4th Row: Purl.
6th Row: K0[0,2,0,0], p0[3,3,0,3], *p2, k3, p3, rep from * to last 7[2,4,7,2] sts, p2, k3[0,2,3,0], p2[0,0,2,0].
8th Row: Purl.
First–8th rows set Yoke Pattern.**
Keeping continuity of pat as set, cont until back measures 28¼[28¼,28¼,29¼, 29½]in (72[72,72,74,75]cm), ending with a WS row.

SHAPE SHOULDERS

Bind off 21[22,22,24,25] sts in pat at beg of next 2 rows. 77[81,85,87,91] sts.
Bind off 21[23,23,24,25] sts in pat at beg of next 2 rows. 35[35,39,39,41] sts.
Leave rem 35[35,39,39,41] sts on a stitch holder.

FRONT

Work as given for Back to **.
Keeping continuity of pat as set,

---

shaping solutions

Once you reach the neck shaping on a garment, each side of the neck is completed separately. The stitches left on a holder at the center front neck are used later for the neckband.

---

cont until front measures 25¼[25¼,25¼, 25½,26]in (64[64,64,65,66]cm), ending with a WS row.

SHAPE NECK

Next Row: Pat 51[54,54,57,59], turn, leave rem 68[71,75,78,82] sts on a stitch holder. Working on these 51[54,54,57,59] sts only, proceed as follows:
Next Row: Work in pat.
Work 4 rows, dec one st at neck edge in every row. 47[50,50,53,55] sts.
Work 9 rows, dec one st at neck edge in next and every foll alt row. 42[45,45,48,50] sts.
Cont without shaping until front measures 28¼[28¼,28¼,29¼,29½]in (72[72,72,74, 75]cm), ending with a WS row.

SHAPE SHOULDER

Next Row: Bind off 21[22,22,24,25] sts in pat, pat to end. 21[23,23,24,25] sts.
Next Row: Work in pat.
Bind off rem 21[23,23,24,25] sts in pat. With RS facing and working on rem 68[71,75,78,82] sts, slip 17[17,21,21, 23] sts onto a stitch holder, rejoin yarn to rem 51[54,54,57,59] sts and pat to end. Complete to match first side of neck reversing shapings.

SLEEVES

Using smaller needles, cast on 53[53,55, 55,59] sts. Work in 1x1 rib for 1½in (4cm), ending with a WS row.

Change to larger needles and proceed as follows:
1st Row: K2[2,3,3,5], *p1, k7, rep from * to last 3[3,4,4,6] sts, p1, k2[2,3,3,5].
2nd Row: Purl.
First and 2nd rows set pat.
Keeping continuity of pat as set, inc 1 st at each end of 3rd and every foll 4th row to 93[89,105,101,111] sts, working inc sts in pat. Inc 1 st at each end of every foll 6th row to 101[101,109,109,115]sts, working inc sts in pat.

techniques

For neckbands, picking up stitches   p. 40

Cont without shaping until sleeve measures 18½[19,19¾,20,20½]in (47[48, 50,51,52]cm), or length required, ending with a WS row.

SHAPE SLEEVE TOP

Bind off 14[14,15,15,16] sts in pat at beg of next 6 rows.
Bind off rem 17[17,19,19,19] sts in pat.

NECKBAND

Join right shoulder seam.
With RS facing and using smaller needles, pick up and knit 23[23,23,25,25] sts evenly along left side of neck, 17[17,21,21, 23] sts left on a stitch holder at front of neck, 24[24,24,26,26] sts evenly along right side of neck, and 35[35,39,39,41] sts left on a stitch holder at back of neck.

99[99,107,111,115] sts.
Starting with 2nd row of 1x1 rib, work 3in (8cm), ending with a WS row.
Bind off loosely in rib.

neat neckline

A doubled-over band gives a neat, professional finish to a crew neckline. To keep the bound-off stitches loose (and stretchy), you can use one size larger needles for the bind-off row.

TO FINISH

Join left shoulder and neckband seams. Fold sleeves in half lengthwise. Placing folds at shoulder seams, sew sleeves in position for approximately 9¾[9¾,10¾, 10¾,11]in (25[25,27,27,28]cm) from top of shoulders. Join side and sleeve seams. Fold neckband in half to WS and slip stitch loosely in position. Pin out garment to the measurements given at right. Cover with damp cloths and allow to dry.

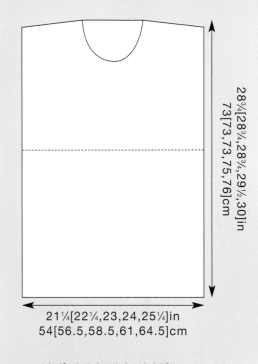

28¾[28¾,28¾,29½,30]in
73[73,73,75,76]cm

21¼[22¼,23,24,25¼]in
54[56.5,58.5,61,64.5]cm

19½[19½,21½,21½,22]in
50[50,54,54,56]cm

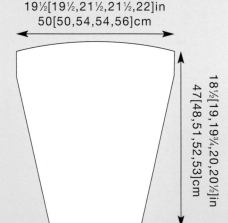

18½[19,19¾,20,20½]in
47[48,51,52,53]cm

baby's hooded sweater

SKILL

1

FOR THE
BEGINNER

JUST PRACTICE YOUR
STOCKINETTE STITCH
AND RIBBING, AND
THEN YOU CAN SHOW
OFF YOUR NEW
KNITTING SKILLS BY
MAKING THIS CUDDLY
SWEATER FOR A NEW
BABY. THE HOOD AND
FRONT POUCH
POCKET GIVE IT A
TRENDY, SPORTY
APPEARANCE.

baby's hooded sweater   **project 5**

baby's hooded sweater

The bouclé baby yarn used for this sweater produces a soft, textured fabric that doesn't show any unevenness in the knitting that is characteristic when new knitters produce stockinette stitch.

MEASUREMENTS

To fit chest	in	16	18	20	22	24	26
	cm	41	46	51	56	61	66
Actual Size	in	19	21¼	23¼	26	28¼	29½
	cm	48	54	59	66	72	75
Length	in	9½	10¾	11½	14	16	18
	cm	24	27	29	36	41	46
Sleeve	in	6	6½	8	9½	11½	13
	cm	15	17	20	24	29	33

Figures in brackets [ ] refer to larger sizes; where there is only one set of figures, it applies to all sizes.

YOU WILL NEED

Number of 50g (1¾oz) skeins Sirdar Snuggly Chatterbox DK (shade 311):

3	3	4	5	6	7

Pair of size 6 (4mm) knitting needles
Pair of size 3 (3¼mm) knitting needles

GAUGE

22 sts and 28 rows to 4in (10cm) over St st on size 6 (4mm) needles or the size required to give the correct gauge.

ABBREVIATIONS

See page 95.

BACK

Using smaller needles, cast on 53[59,65, 73,79,83] sts.
Work 6 rows in k1, p1 rib.
Change to larger needles. Work in St st until back measures 5¼[6,6,8¼,9¾,11]in (13[15,15,21,25,28]cm), ending with a WS row.

simple measuring

Measure stockinette stitch on the wrong side of the work, using a line of purl stitches as a guide.

SHAPE ARMHOLES

Bind off 6 sts at beg of next 2 rows.**
41[47,53,61,67,71] sts.
Cont without shaping until armholes measure 4[4¼,5¼,5½,6,6½]in (10[11,13, 14,15,17]cm), ending with a WS row.

SHAPE SHOULDERS

Bind off 5[6,7,9,10,11] sts at beg of next 2 rows. 31[35,39,43,47,49] sts. Bind off 5[7,8,10,11,12] sts at beg of next 2 rows. Bind off rem 21[21,23,23,25,25] sts.

FRONT

Work as given for Back to **.
41[47,53,61,67,71] sts.
Cont without shaping until armholes measure 2[2½,3,3,3½,4¼]in (5[6,8,8, 9,11]cm), ending with a WS row.

techniques ▶

For stockinette
stitch   p. 17

Shape Neck

Next Row: K15[18,20,24,26,28], turn and leave rem 26[29,33,37,41,43] sts on a stitch holder.
Working on these 15[18,20,24,26,28] sts only, cont as follows:
Next Row: Purl.
Work 2 rows, dec one st at neck edge in every row. 13[16,18,22,24,26] sts. Work 5 rows, dec one st at neck edge in next and every foll alt row. 10[13,15,19,21,23] sts. Cont without shaping until armhole measures 4[4¼,5¼,5½,6,6½]in (10[11,13,14,15,17]cm), ending with a WS row.

Shape Shoulder

Next Row: Bind off 5[6,7,9,10,11] sts, knit to end. 5[7,8,10,11,12] sts.
Next Row: Purl.
Bind off rem 5[7,8,10,11,12] sts.
With RS facing and working on rem 26[29,33,37,41,43] sts, cont as follows:
Next Row: Bind off 11[11,13,13,15,15] sts, knit to end. 15[18,20,24,26,28] sts.
Complete to match first side of neck, reversing shapings.

Sleeves

Using smaller needles, cast on 31[31,33, 33,37,39] sts.

Work in k1, p1 rib for 1¼[1¼,1¼,1½,1½,1½]in (3[3,3,4,4,4]cm), ending with a RS row.
Next Row: Rib 3[3,4,4,6,7], m1, (rib 5, m1) 5 times, rib 3[3,4,4,6,7]. 37[37,39, 39,43,45] sts.
Change to larger needles. Working in St st throughout, inc one st at each end of 5th and every foll 6th[4th,4th,4th, 6th,5th] row to 45[51,57,61,63,73] sts. Cont without shaping until sleeve measures 7[8,9,10¾,12½,14]in (18[20, 23,27,32,36]cm), ending with a WS row. Bind off.

Hood

Using larger needles, cast on 68[72,72,76, 84,86] sts. Working in St st throughout, cont until hood measures 6[6½,7,7½, 8,8¼]in (15[17,18,19,20,21]cm), ending with a WS row.

headline news

The hood of this garment is knitted separately and sewn in place around the neck edge of the sweater afterward.

Shape Top

Bind off 23[24,24,25,28,28] sts, k21[23,23,25,27,29], bind off 23[24,24, 25,28,28] sts.
With WS facing, rejoin yarn to rem 22[24,24,26,28,30] sts and purl to end. Cont without shaping until hood measures 4[4¼,4¼,4¾,5¼,5¼]in (10[11,11, 12,13,13]cm) from bound-off sts, ending with a WS row. Bind off.

Hood Border

Join hood seams.
Using smaller needles and with RS facing, pick up and knit 33[38,40,43,46,47] sts evenly along right side of hood, 21[23, 23,25,27,29] sts from top of hood, and 33[38,40,43,46,47] sts evenly along left side of hood. 87[99,103,111,119,123] sts. Work 5 rows in k1, p1 rib.
Bind off in rib.

techniques

For decreases   p. 20
For increases   p. 22

MEASUREMENTS

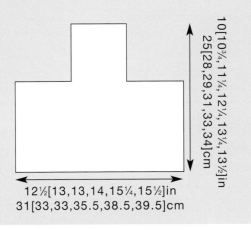

10[10¾,11¼,12¼,13¼,13½]in
25[28,29,31,33,34]cm

12½[13,13,14,15¼,15½]in
31[33,33,35.5,38.5,39.5]cm

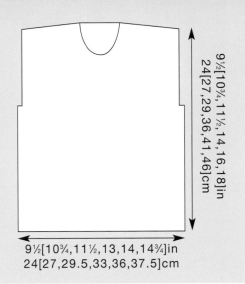

9½[10¾,11½,14,16,18]in
24[27,29,36,41,46]cm

9½[10¾,11½,13,14,14¾]in
24[27,29.5,33,36,37.5]cm

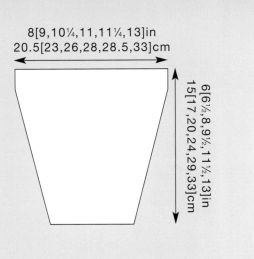

8[9,10¼,11,11¼,13]in
20.5[23,26,28,28.5,33]cm

6[6½,8,9¼,11½,13]in
15[17,20,24,29,33]cm

POCKET

Using larger needles, cast on 42[46, 46,50,50,54] sts. Working in St st throughout, work 14[14,18,18,22,22] rows.

SHAPE TOP

For first, 2nd, 3rd, 4th and 5th sizes only
1st Row: K2, sl1-k1-psso, knit to last 4 sts, k2tog, k2.
2nd Row: K2, p2tog, purl to last 4 sts, p2tog tbl, k2. 38[42,42,46,46] sts.
Rep first and 2nd rows 5[3,3,1,1] times. 18[30,30,42,42] sts.
Then proceed as follows:

For all 6 sizes
1st Row: K2, sl1-k1-psso, knit to last 4 sts, k2tog, k2.
2nd Row: K2, purl to last 2 sts, k2.
Rep first and 2nd rows 1[5,5,7,7,11] times more.
Bind off rem 14[18,18,26,26,30] sts.

TO FINISH

Press as directed on yarn label. Join shoulder seams. Sew in sleeves, sewing row ends at top of sleeves to bound-off sts at underarms. Sew pocket in position at center of front above rib. With ends of hood border to center of front neck, sew on hood. Join side and sleeve seams.

hidden stitches

When sewing the pocket to the front of the sweater, use a neat slip stitch. The stitch threads will sink into the knitted fabric, making them invisible.

terrific textures

A knitted fabric with a wonderful texture is a joy to look at and to wear. Use cables and crisp Aran patterns for smart cushions and a throw. Dress up in a beautiful openwork lace scarf. Stay elegantly casual in a cozy patchwork-style sweater. Or have fun in a jacket with loopy edgings. And don't forget the kids — make them super jackets with top designer class.

lacy scarf

LIGHT AND FEATHERY
IN A BEAUTIFUL 4-PLY
SILK YARN, THIS
LACE-PATTERNED
SCARF IS AN
IDEAL ACCESSORY
FOR ELEGANT
EVENING WEAR.
THE LUXURIOUS
FRINGE IS TRIMMED
WITH HUNDREDS OF
TINY BEADS.

lacy scarf **project 6**

lacy scarf

You can knit this scarf from just one small skein of silk yarn. Large needles help to keep the lace pattern light and airy and ensure that your scarf grows in no time at all.

MEASUREMENTS

Finished scarf measures approximately 8in (20cm) wide by 38in (96cm) long, excluding fringe

YOU WILL NEED

Number of 50g (1¾oz) skeins Jaeger Silk: 1 skein (shade 131)

Pair of size 6 (4mm) knitting needles
Pair of size 7 (4½mm) knitting needles
360 small glass beads

GAUGE

22 sts and 23 rows to 4in (10cm) over pattern on size 7 (4½mm) needles or the size required to give the correct gauge.

ABBREVIATIONS

See page 95.

FRINGE

For fringe, cut 90 lengths of yarn, each 5in (12cm) long, and put to one side.

SCARF

Using smaller needles, cast on 45 sts.
Work in garter st (knit every row) for 4 rows, ending with a WS row.
Change to larger needles.
Work in lacy pat as follows:
1st Row: (RS) K5, *k2tog, yo, k1, yo, sl1-k1-psso, k5, rep from * to end.
2nd and Every Alt Row: K2, p to last 2 sts, k2.
3rd Row: K4, *k2tog, (k1, yo) twice, k1, sl1-k1-psso, k3, rep from * to last st, k1.
5th Row: K3, *k2tog, k2, yo, k1, yo, k2, sl1-k1-psso, k1, rep from * to last 2 sts, k2.
7th Row: K2, k2tog, *k3, yo, k1, yo, k3, sl1-k2tog-psso, rep from * to last 11 sts, k3, yo, k1, yo, k3, sl1-k1-psso, k2.
9th Row: K3, *yo, sl1-k1-psso, k5, k2tog, yo, k1, rep from * to last 2 sts, k2.
11th Row: K3, *yo, k1, sl1-k1-psso, k3, k2tog, k1, yo, k1, rep from * to last 2 sts, k2.
13th Row: K3, *yo, k2, sl1-k1-psso, k1, k2tog, k2, yo, k1, rep from * to last 2 sts, k2.

15th Row: K3, *yo, k3, sl1-k2tog-psso, k3, yo, k1, rep from * to last 2 sts, k2.
16th Row: As 2nd row.
These 16 rows form pat. Cont in pat until almost all the yarn has been used up, ending after a 7th or 15th pat row and allowing sufficient yarn to work 3 rows more and bind off. (If required, adjust scarf length here.)
Change to smaller needles. Work in garter st for 3 rows, ending with a WS row. Bind off.

TO FINISH

Press carefully, following instructions on yarn label. Attach fringe along short ends, knotting one folded length of the cut yarn into each st. Thread 2 beads onto each strand of the fringe and knot yarn end to secure beads.

woman's chunky sweater

woman's chunky sweater **project 7**

SKILL

2

PRACTICE
MAKES
PERFECT

KEEP SNUG AND
WARM IN THE
COLDEST WEATHER
IN THIS CHUNKY
SWEATER WITH ITS
ROLLED RIB COLLAR.
PANELS OF
STOCKINETTE AND
REVERSE
STOCKINETTE FORM A
PATCHWORK OF
TWISTED STITCH
PATTERNS.

woman's chunky sweater

This is the perfect sweater to make as an introduction to working twisted stitch patterns. The pattern panel instructions are written separately, so practice them first, and the bulky yarn will knit up quickly and easily.

MEASUREMENTS

To Fit bust				
	in	34-36	38-40	42-44
	cm	86-91	97-102	107-112
Actual Size	in	41¾	45¾	49¾
	cm	106	116	126
Length	in	23¼	23¼	23¼
	cm	59	59	59
Sleeve	in	18	18	18
	cm	46	46	46

Figures in brackets [ ] refer to larger sizes; where there is only one set of figures, it applies to all sizes.

YOU WILL NEED

Number of 100g (3½oz) skeins Sirdar Super Nova	6	6	6

Pair of size 11 (8mm) knitting keedles
Pair of size 10 (6mm) knitting needles

GAUGE

12 sts and 16 rows to 4in (10cm) over pattern on size 11 (8mm) needles or size required to achieve correct gauge.

ABBREVIATIONS

See page 95.

PATTERN PANEL I

1st Row: K21[23,25].
2nd Row: P21[23,25].
3rd Row: K9[10,11], p1, k1, p1, k9[10,11].
4th Row: P8[9,10], k2, p1, k2, p8[9,10].
5th Row: K7[8,9], p2, k3, p2, k7[8,9].
6th Row: P6[7,8], k2, p5, k2, p6[7,8].
7th Row: K5[6,7], p2, k2, p1, k1, p1, k2, p2, k5[6,7].
8th Row: P2[3,4], (p2, k2) twice, p1, (k2, p2) twice, p2[3,4].
9th Row: K3[4,5], (p2, k2) twice, k1, (p2, k2) twice, k1[2,3].
10th Row: P3[4,5], k1, p2, k2, p5, k2, p2, k1, p3[4,5].
11th and 12th Rows: As 7th and 8th rows.

13th Row: K4[5,6], p1, k2, p2, k3, p2, k2, p1, k4[5,6].
14th and 15th Rows: As 6th and 7th rows.
16th Row: P5[6,7], k1, p2, k2, p1, k2, p2, k1, p5[6,7].
17th and 18th Rows: As 5th and 6th rows.
19th Row: K6[7,8], p1, k2, p1, k1, p1, k2, p1, k6[7,8].
20th and 21st Rows: As 4th and 5th rows.
22nd Row: P7[8,9], (k1, p5) twice, p2[3,4].
23rd and 24th Rows: As 3rd and 4th rows.
25th Row: K8[9,10], p1, k3, p1, k8[9,10].
26th and 27th Rows: As 2nd and 3rd rows.
28th Row: P9[10,11], k1, p1, k1, p9[10,11].
29th Row: As first row.
30th Row: P21[23,25].
First–30th rows set pat.

PATTERN PANEL II

1st Row: P21[23,25].
2nd Row: K21[23,25].
3rd Row: As first row.
4th Row: K5[6,7], (p1, k4) twice, p1, k5[6,7].
5th Row: P5[6,7], purl into the back of the 2nd st on left-hand needle then knit into front of the first st on left-hand needle, slip both sts off needle tog (this will now be referred to as T2F), p3, k1tbl, p3, knit into the front of the 2nd st on left-hand needle then purl into the front of first st on left-hand needle, slip both sts off needle tog (this will now be referred to as T2B), p5[6,7].
6th Row: K6[7,8], p1, (k3, p1) twice, k6[7,8].
7th Row: P6[7,8], T2F, p2, k1tbl, p2, T2B, p6[7,8].

8th Row: K7[8,9], p1, (k2, p1) twice, k7[8,9].
9th Row: P7[8,9], T2F, p1, k1tbl, p1, T2B, p7[8,9].
10th Row: K8[9,10], p1, (k1, p1) twice, k8[9,10].
11th Row: P8[9,10], T2F, k1tbl, T2B, p8[9,10].
12th Row: As 4th row.
13th–20th Rows: As 5th–12th rows.
21st–27th Rows: As 5th–11th rows.
28th Row: As 2nd row.
29th Row: As first row.
30th Row: K21[23,25].
First–30th rows set pat.

BACK

Using smaller needles, cast on 74[82, 86] sts.
1st Row: K2, *p2, k2, rep from * to end.
2nd Row: *P2, k2, rep from * to last 2 sts, p2.

easy patchwork

Because this sweater is knitted in a single color, there's no need to join in a new color to create patches. The patchwork effect is formed with alternating smooth and textured backgrounds.

These 2 rows will now be referred to as 2x2 rib. Work in 2x2 rib for 1in (2.5cm), ending with a RS row.

For first size only

Next Row: Rib 6, *k2tog, p2, k2, p2tog, k2, p2, rep from * to last 8 sts, k2tog, rib 6. 63 sts.

For 2nd and 3rd sizes only

Next Row: Rib [4,12], *p2tog, k2, p2, k2tog, p2, k2, rep from * to last [6,14] sts, p2tog, rib [4,12]. [69,75] sts.

For all 3 sizes

Change to larger needles and proceed as follows:***
**1st Row: Pat 21[23,25] sts as given for first row of Pat 2, pat 21[23,25] sts as given for first row of Pat 1, pat 21[23,25] sts as given for first row of Pat 2.
2nd Row: Pat 21[23,25] sts as given for 2nd row of Pat 2, pat 21[23,25] sts as given for 2nd row of Pat 1, pat 21[23, 25] sts as given for 2nd row of Pat 2. First and 2nd rows set pat. Keeping continuity of pat as set and starting with 3rd row of Pats 2 and 1, work 28 rows more.

techniques ▶

For casting on   p. 10

For traveling stitches   p. 29

31st Row: Pat 21[23,25] sts as given for first row of Pat 1, pat 21[23,25] sts as given for first row of Pat 2, pat 21[23, 25] sts as given for first row of Pat 1.

32nd Row: Pat 21[23,25] sts as given for 2nd row of Pat 1, pat 21[23,25] sts as given for 2nd row of Pat 2, pat 21[23, 25] sts as given for 2nd row of Pat 1. 31st and 32nd rows set pat. Keeping continuity of pat as set and starting with 3rd row of Pats 1 and 2, work 28 rows more.**

From ** to ** sets pat.

Keeping continuity of pat as set (throughout), work 24 rows more.

SHAPE SHOULDERS

Bind off 7[8,8] sts in pat at beg of next 2 rows. 49[53,59] sts.

Bind off 7[8,9] sts in pat at beg of next 2 rows. 35[37,41] sts.

Bind off 8[8,9] sts in pat at beg of next 2 rows. 19[21,23] sts.

Cut off yarn and leave rem 19[21,23] sts on a stitch holder.

FRONT

Work as given for Back to ***.

****1st Row:** Pat 21[23,25] sts as given for first row of Pat 1, pat 21[23,25] sts as given for first row of Pat 2, pat 21[23,25] sts as given for first row of Pat 1.

2nd Row: Pat 21[23,25] sts as given for 2nd row of Pat 1, pat 21[23,25] sts as given for 2nd row of Pat 2, pat 21[23, 25] sts as given for 2nd row of Pat 1. First and 2nd rows set pat.

Keeping continuity of pat as set and starting with 3rd row of Pats 1 and 2, work 28 rows more.

31st Row: Pat 21[23,25] sts as given for first row of Pat 2, pat 21[23,25] sts as given for first row of Pat 1, pat 21[23, 25] sts as given for first row of Pat 2.

32nd Row: Pat 21[23,25] sts as given for 2nd row of Pat 2, pat 21[23,25] sts as given for 2nd row of Pat 1, pat 21[23, 25] sts as given for 2nd row of Pat 2. 31st and 32nd rows set pat.

Keeping continuity of pat as set and starting with 3rd row of Pats 2 and 1, work 28 rows more.**

From ** to ** sets pat.

Work 16 rows more in pat.

SHAPE LEFT NECK

Next Row: Pat 25[27,29], turn, leave rem 38[42,46] sts on a stitch holder.

Working on these 25[27,29] sts only proceed as follows:

Next Row: Work in pat.

Work 3 rows, dec one st at neck edge in every row. 22[24,26] sts. Work 3 rows even.

SHAPE LEFT SHOULDER

Next Row: Bind off 7[8,8] sts in pat, pat to end. 15[16,18] sts.

Next Row: Work in pat.

Next Row: Bind off 7[8,9] sts in pat, pat to end. 8[8,9] sts.

Next Row: Work in pat.

Bind off rem 8[8,9] sts in pat.

SHAPE RIGHT NECK

With RS facing, work on rem 38[42,46] sts. Slip 13[15,17] sts onto a holder, rejoin yarn to rem 25[27,29] sts and pat to end.

Next Row: Work in pat.

Work 3 rows, dec one st at neck edge in every row. 22[24,26] sts.

Work 4 rows even.

techniques ▶

For decreases   p. 20-21

SHAPE RIGHT SHOULDER

Next Row: Bind off 7[8,8] sts in pat, pat to end. 15[16,18] sts.

Next Row: Work in pat.

Next Row: Bind off 7[8,9] sts in pat, pat to end. 8[8,9] sts.

Next Row: Work in pat.

Bind off rem 8[8,9] sts.

SLEEVES

Using smaller needles, cast on 30[34, 34] sts. Work in 2x2 rib for 1½[1½,2]in (4[4,5]cm), ending with a RS row.

Next Row: Rib to end, inc one st at center of row. 31[35,35] sts.

Change to larger needles and proceed as follows:

1st Row: P5[6,5], pat 21[23,25] sts as given for first row of Pat 1, p5[6,5].

2nd Row: K5[6,5], pat 21[23,25] sts as given for 2nd row of Pat 1, k5[6,5].

First and 2nd rows set pat.

Keeping continuity of pat as set and starting with 3rd row of Pat 1, work 28 rows, inc one st at each end of next and every foll 6th[8th,6th] row until there are 41[43,45] sts, working increased sts in Pat 2.

31st Row: K10, pat 21[23,25] sts as given for first row of Pat 2, k10.

32nd Row: P10, pat 21[23,25] sts as given for 2nd row of Pat 2, p10.

31st and 32nd rows set pat.

Keeping continuity of pat as set, work 25[27,25] rows, inc one st at each end of 1st[3rd,1st] and every foll 6th[8th,6th] row until there are 51[51,55] sts, working increased sts in Pat 1.

Work 3[1,3] rows even.

These 60 rows set pat.

Keeping continuity of pat as set, work even until sleeve measures 18in (46cm), or length required, ending with a WS row.

Bind off in pat.

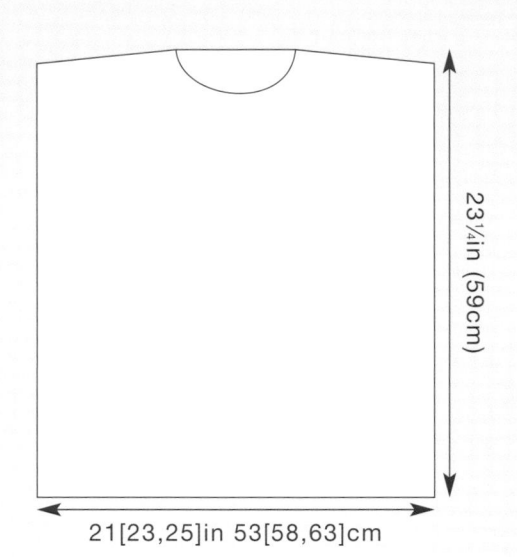

23¼in (59cm)

21[23,25]in 53[58,63]cm

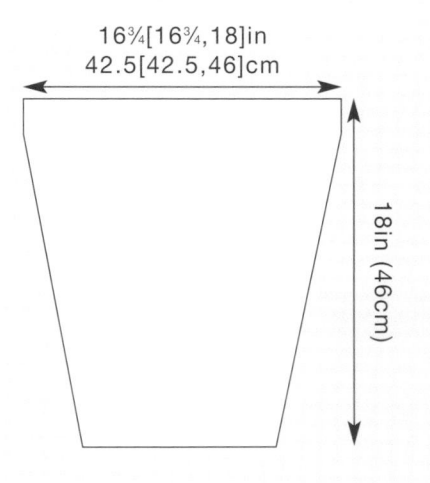

16¾[16¾,18]in
42.5[42.5,46]cm

18in (46cm)

TURTLENECK

Join right shoulder seam.
With RS facing and using larger needles, pick up and knit 13 sts evenly along left side of neck, 13[15,17] sts left on stitch holder at front of neck, 13 sts evenly along right side of neck, and 19[21,23] sts left on stitch holder at back of neck. 58[62,66] sts.
Starting with first row of 2x2 rib, work 7in (18cm), ending with a WS row.
Bind off loosely in rib.

TO FINISH

Pin out garment to measurements on page 36. Cover with damp cloths and allow to dry. Join left shoulder and neckband seams, reversing sewing for turtleneck. Fold sleeves in half lengthwise, and with folds at shoulder seams, sew sleeves 8¼[8¼,9]in (21[21,23]cm) down from tops of shoulders. Join side and sleeve seams.

counting rows

If you find it hard to keep track of the rows when you are shaping the sleeves, invest in a row counter. This simple device fits onto the end of one of your needles, and with a simple click you can move it on at the end of every row. Alternatively mark the rows on a piece of paper.

THESE ARAN
CUSHIONS AND
THROW, KNITTED IN
COTTON AND ICE-
CREAM COLORS,
FEATURE INTRICATE
CABLES AGAINST A
CRISP-TEXTURED
BACKGROUND.
THE CUSHIONS ARE
TRIMMED WITH
KNITTED CORD THAT
TIES IN A BOW AT
EACH CORNER.

SKILL

3

ENJOY THE
CHALLENGE

aran cushions
and throw

aran cushions and throw

These cushion covers are ideal for practicing your Aran techniques. Because they are worked as flat pieces, you won't need to worry about creating the cable pattern and shaping the fabric all at the same time.

MEASUREMENTS

Finished cushion cover fits a 12[16]in (30[40]cm) square pillow form

Finished throw measures approximately 48 x 57in (123 x 146cm)

Cushion instructions are for a 12in (30cm) square pillow form. Figures in brackets [ ] refer to a 16in (40cm) square pillow form. Where there is only one set of figures, it applies to both sizes.

YOU WILL NEED

Number of 50g (1¾oz) skeins Rowan Handknit DK Cotton:
Small cushion   8 skeins (shade 203)
Large cushion 12 skeins (shade 204)
Throw   32 skeins (shade 209)

Pair of size 3 (3¼mm) knitting needles
Pair of size 6 (4mm) knitting needles
2 double-pointed size 3 (3¼mm) knitting needles
Cable needle

GAUGE

20 sts and 28 rows to 4in (10cm) over St st on size 6 (4mm) needles or the size required to give the correct gauge.

ABBREVIATIONS

See page 95.
C8B = Cable 8 back: Slip next 4 sts onto cable needle and leave at back of work, k4, then k4 from cable needle.
C9B = Cable 9 back: Slip next 5 sts onto cable needle and leave at back of work, k4, slip p st from cable needle back onto left needle and p this st, then k4 from cable needle.
C9F = Cable 9 front: Slip next 5 sts onto cable needle and leave at front of work, k4, slip p st from cable needle back onto left needle and p this st, then k4 from cable needle.

CUSHION PANELS (MAKE 2)

Using larger needles, cast on 81[101] sts.
1st Row: (RS) K1, (p1, k1) 3[8] times, work next 67 sts as first row of cushion chart, (k1, p1) 3[8] times, k1.
2nd Row: K1, (p1, k1) 3[8] times, work next 67 sts as 2nd row of cushion chart, (k1, p1) 3[8] times, k1.
These 2 rows set the sts—center 67 sts in pat foll chart (on page 40) with edge sts in seed st. Keeping sts correct as set and repeating the 28 pat rows throughout, cont without shaping until panel measures 12[16]in (30[40]cm), ending with a WS row. Bind off.
Place two cushion panels together with WS facing.

techniques ▶

For cables   p. 28

For picking up stitches   p. 40

□ = k on RS, p on WS

• = p on RS, k on WS

⟋⟋⟋⟋ = C8B

⟋⟋⟋⟋ = C9B

⟍⟍ ⟍ = C9F

CUSHION EDGING

With RS facing, using smaller needles, and working through edge of both panels together, pick up and knit 64[84] sts along first side.

Beg with a k row, work in reverse St st for 8 rows.

Bind off.

Work edging along other 3 sides of the cushion in same way, remembering to insert pillow form before working edging along fourth side.

Allow the edging to roll over to the pick-up row and neatly slip stitch in place to form casing. This is where the ties will be threaded through.

TIES (MAKE 4)

Using double-pointed needles, cast on 4 sts.

Next Row: (RS) K4 (all 4 sts now on right needle), *slip sts to opposite end of

needle and transfer this needle to left hand, without turning work and taking yarn quite tightly across back of work, k same 4 sts again (all 4 sts now on right needle again), rep from * until tie is 36[40]in (90[100]cm) long. Bind off. Thread ties through rolled casings and tie in bows at corners.

tubular ties

Using two double-pointed needles to make the ties produces a long, tubular strip of fabric. For more detailed instructions on this form of knitting in the round, see the techniques book, page 26.

THROW

Using smaller needles cast on 244 sts. Work 7 rows in garter st (knit every row).

Next Row: (inc row) K20, *(m1, k1) 4 times, k15*, rep from * to * 4 times more, (k1, m1) 13 times, k18, rep from * to * 5 times, k3. 297 sts.
Change to larger needles.

1st Row: (RS) K5, (p1, k1) 7 times, (work next 23 sts of side panel as indicated on first row of throw chart) 5 times, work next 29 sts of center panel as indicated on first row of chart, (work next 23 sts of side panel as indicated on first row of chart) 5 times, (k1, p1) 7 times, k5.

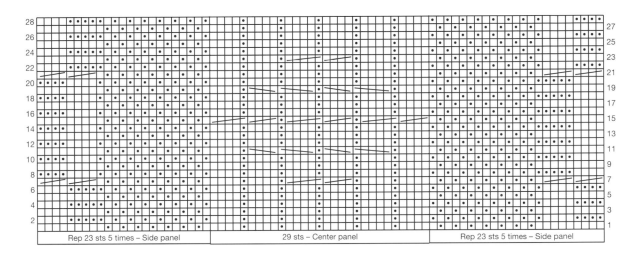

Rep 23 sts 5 times – Side panel	29 sts – Center panel

Rep 23 sts 5 times – Side panel

T H R O W   C H A R T

2nd Row: K5, (p1, k1) 7 times, (work next 23 sts of side panel as indicated on 2nd row of throw chart) 5 times, work next 29 sts of center panel as indicated on 2nd

row of chart, (work next 23 sts of side panel as indicated on 2nd row chart) 5 times, (k1, p1) 7 times, k5.

These 2 rows set the sts—115-st side panels at either side of center 29 sts, with seed st borders and garter st edgings. Keeping sts correct as set, repeat the 28 pat rows 12 times more, then work first-27th rows again.

Next Row: (dec row) K19, *(k2tog) 4 times, k15*, rep from * to * 4 more times, k2, (k2tog) 13 times, k16, rep from * to * 5 more times, k4. 244 sts.
Change to smaller needles.
Work 7 rows in garter st. Bind off.

K E Y

□ = k on RS, p on WS

• = p on RS, k on WS

= C8B

= C9B

= C9F

techniques ▶

For garter stitch   p. 17

For increases   p. 22

baby's textured jacket

EVEN THE VERY
YOUNGEST OF US
DESERVES TO BE
DRESSED IN THE
LATEST KNITTED
FASHIONS. THIS
JACKET, WITH ITS
NEAT COLLAR,
COMBINES A
COLLECTION OF
STITCH PATTERNS,
CABLES, AND STRIPES
IN A PLEASING PASTEL
COLORWAY.

SKILL

3

ENJOY THE
CHALLENGE

baby's textured jacket

Try knitting this snazzy jacket as a change from usual baby outfits. You'll need to be a confident knitter for the variety of stitch and pattern work using the intarsia technique, but the finished result is worth the effort.

MEASUREMENTS

To fit chest	in	16	18	20	22	24
	cm	41	46	51	56	61
Actual Size	in	18	20½	22½	25	27
	cm	46	52	58	64	69
Length	in	9½	10¼	12	14	16½
	cm	24	26	31	36	42
Sleeve	in	6	6½	8	9½	11½
	cm	15	17	20	24	29

Figures in brackets [ ] refer to larger sizes; where there is only one set of figures, it applies to all sizes.

YOU WILL NEED

Number of 50g (1¾oz) skeins Sirdar Snuggly Baby Care DK:

A (339)	1	1	2	2	2
B (340)	1	1	2	2	2
C (208)	1	1	2	2	2

Pair of size 6 (4mm) knitting needles
Pair of size 3 (3¼mm) knitting needles
Cable needle (CN)
5[5,6,6,7] buttons

GAUGE

One cable panel (10 sts) measures 1¼in (3cm).
21 sts and 28 rows to 4in (10cm) over pattern and moss stitch on size 6 (4mm) needles or the size required to give the correct gauge.

ABBREVIATIONS

See page 95.

Intarsia technique

When working with different skeins of yarn, the color to be used should be twisted around the color just used to link the colors together and avoid holes. Do not join in and break off colors, except where necessary.

BACK

Using larger needles and A, cast on 49[55,61,67,73] sts.
1st Row: Knit.

Cont in garter st (knit every row), work 7[7,7,9,9] rows. Proceed as follows:

For 4th and 5th sizes only
1st Row: Using B, knit.
2nd Row: Using B, purl.
These 2 rows will now be referred to as St st (stockinette stitch).
Work [0,2] rows more in St st.

For all 5 sizes
Using B, proceed as follows:
1st and Every Alt Row: Knit.
2nd Row: P0[0,3,0,0], k0[1,1,0,1], p2[4,4,2,4], *p4, k1, p4, rep from * to last 2[5,8,2,5] sts, p2[4,4,2,4], k0[1,1,0,1], p0[0,3,0,0].
4th Row: P0[0,2,0,0], k0[2,3,0,2], p2[3,3,2,3], *p3, k3, p3, rep from * to last 2[5,8,2,5] sts, p2[3,3,2,3], k0[2,3,0,2], p0[0,2,0,0].

6th Row: P0[0,1,0,0], k0[3,5,0,3], p2, *p2, k5, p2, rep from * to last 2[5,8,2,5] sts, p2, k0[3,5,0,3], p0[1,0,0,0].

8th Row: K0[4,7,0,4], p2[1,1,2,1], *p1, k7, p1, rep from * to last 2[5,8,2,5]sts, p2[1,1,2,1], k0[4,7,0,4].

10th Row: K0[0,3,0,0], p0[1,1,0,1], k0[3,3,0,3], p2[1,1,2,1], *(p1, k3) twice, p1, rep from * to last 2[5,8,2,5] sts, p2[1,1,2,1], k0[3,3,0,3], p0[1,1,0,1], k0[0,3,0,0].

12th Row: (P1, k1, p1) 0[0,1,0,0] times, p0[2,2,0,2], k0[1,1,0,1], p2, *p2, k1, p3, k1, p2, rep from * to last 2[5,8,2,5] sts, p2, k0[1,1,0,1], p0[2,2,0,2], (p1, k1, p1) 0[0,1,0,0] times.
Work 0[0,0,2,4] rows in St st.

Using A, work 3 rows in garter st.
Next Row: Using A, k10[12,14,16,18], pick up loop between last and next st and work into the back of this loop (this will now be referred to as m1), (k1, m1) 3 times, k23[25,27,29,31], m1, (k1, m1) 3 times, k10[12,14,16,18]. 57[63,69,75,81] sts.
Proceed as follows:

1st Row: K9[11,13,15,17]C; using A, p1, slip next 2 sts to back on CN, k2 then k2 from CN (this will now be referred to as C4B), slip next 2 sts to front on CN, k2 then k2 from CN (this will now be referred to as C4F), p1; k19[21,23,25, 27]C; using A, p1, C4B, C4F, p1; k9[11, 13,15,17]C.

2nd Row: Using C, (k1, p1) 4[5,6,7,8] times, k1; k1A, p8A, k1A; p19[21,23,25, 27]C; k1A, p8A, k1A; using C, k1, (p1, k1) 4[5,6,7,8] times.

3rd Row: Using C, (k1, p1) 4[5,6,7,8] times, k1; p1A, k8A, p1A; k19[21,23,25, 27]B; p1A, k8A, p1A; using C, k1, (p1, k1) 4[5,6,7,8] times.

4th Row: Using C, (p1, k1) 4[5,6,7,8] times, p1; k1A, p8A, k1A; p19[21,23,25, 27]B; k1A, p8A, k1A; using C, p1, (k1, p1) 4[5,6,7,8] times.

5th Row: Using C, (p1, k1) 4[5,6,7,8] times, p1; using A, p1, C4F, C4B, p1; k19[21,23,25,27]C; using A, p1, C4F, C4B, p1; using C, p1, (k1, p1) 4[5,6,7,8] times.
The 2nd–5th rows set moss-st panels at side edges.

6th Row: As 2nd row.

7th Row: As 3rd row.

8th Row: Using C, (p1, k1) 4[5,6,7,8] times, p1; k1A, p8A, k1A; p19[21,23,25, 27]B; k1A, p8A, k1A; using C, p1, (k1, p1) 4[5,6,7,8] times.
First–8th rows set cable panel and striped panel.
Keeping continuity of pat panels as set, work 6[6,14,22,30] rows more in pat.

Next Row: Using A, k10[12,14,16,18], (k2tog) 4 times, k21[23,25,27,29], (k2tog) 4 times, k10[12,14,16,18]. 49[55,61, 67,73] sts.
Using A, work 3 rows in garter st. Using B only throughout, proceed as follows:

techniques

For cables   p. 28

SHAPE ARMHOLES

Next Row: Bind off 4 sts, knit to end.
Next Row: Bind off 4 sts purlwise, p2[5,0, 3,0], (k1, p5) 0[0,0,0,1] times, *k1, p1, k1, p5, rep from * to last 6[9,4,7,2] sts, k1, p1, k1[1,1,1,0], p3[6,1,4,0]. 41[47,53,59,65] sts.
Proceed as follows:
1st Row: Knit.
2nd Row: P3[6,1,4,1], (k1, p5) 0[0,0,0,1] times, *k1, p1, k1, p5, rep from * to last 6[9,4,7,2] sts, k1, p1, k1[1,1,1,0], p3[6,1,4,0].
First and 2nd rows set pat. Keeping

continuity of pat as set, cont until armholes measure 4[4¾,5¼,5½,6]in (10[12, 13,14,15]cm), ending with a WS row.

SHAPE SHOULDERS

Bind off 5[7,8,9,10] sts in pat at beg of next 2 rows. 31[33,37,41,45] sts.
Bind off 6[7,8,10,11] sts in pat at beg of next 2 rows. 19[19,21,21,23] sts.
Bind off rem 19[19,21,21,23] sts in pat.

LEFT FRONT

Using larger needles and A, cast on 22[25,28,31,34] sts, and work 8[8,8,10,10] rows in garter st.
Proceed as follows:

For 4th and 5th sizes only
Using B, work [2,4] rows in St st.

For all 5 sizes
Using B, proceed as follows:
**1st and Every Alt Row: Knit.
2nd Row: P2, *p4, k1, p4, rep from * to last 2[5,8,2,5] sts, p2[4,4,2,4], k0[1,1,0,1], p0[0,3,0,0].
4th Row: P2, *p3, k3, p3, rep from * to last 2[5,8,2,5] sts, p2[3,3,2,3], k0[2,3,0,2], p0[0,2,0,0].
6th Row: P2, *p2, k5, p2, rep from * to last 2[5,8,2,5] sts, p2, k0[3,5,0,3], p0[0,1,0,0].
8th Row: P2, *p1, k7, p1, rep from * to last 2[5,8,2,5] sts, p2[1,1,2,1], k0[4,7,0,4].
10th Row: P2, *(p1, k3) twice, p1, rep from * to last 2[5,8,2,5] sts, p2[1,1,2,1], k0[3,3,0,3], p0[1,1,0,1], k0[0,3,0,0].
12th Row: P2, *p2, k1, p3, k1, p2, rep from * to last 2[5,8,2,5] sts, p2, k0[1,1,0,1], p0[2,2,0,2], (p1, k1, p1) 0[0,1,0,0] times.
Work 0[0,0,2,4] rows in St st.
Using A, work 3 rows in garter st.
Next Row: Using A, k9[10,11,12,13], m1, (k1, m1) 3 times, k10[12,14,16,18].

26[29,32,35,38] sts.
Proceed as follows:

1st Row: K9[11,13,15,17]C; using A, p1,
C4B, C4F, p1; k7[8,9,10,11]C.

2nd Row: P7[8,9,10,11]C; k1A, p8A, k1A;
using C, k1, (p1, k1) 4[5,6,7,8] times.

3rd Row: Using C, (k1, p1) 4[5,6,7,8]
times, k1; p1A, k8A, p1A; k7[8,9,10,11]B.

4th Row: P7[8,9,10,11]B; k1A, p8A, k1A;
using C, p1, (k1, p1) 4[5,6,7,8] times.

5th Row: Using C, (p1, k1) 4[5,6,7,8] times,
p1; using A, p1, C4F, C4B, p1; k7[8,9,
10,11]C.

The 2nd–5th rows set moss-st panel at
side edge.

6th and 7th Rows: As 2nd and 3rd rows.

8th Row: P7[8,9,10,11]B; k1A, p8A, k1A;
using C, p1, (k1, p1) 4[5,6,7,8] times.

First–8th rows set cable panel and
striped panel.

Keeping continuity of pat panels as set,
work 6[6,14,22,30] rows more in pat.

Next Row: Using A, k10[12,14,16,18],
(k2tog) 4 times, k8[9,10,11,12]. 22[25,28,
31,34] sts.

Using A, work 3 rows in garter st. Using B
only throughout, proceed as follows:

SHAPE ARMHOLE

Next Row: Bind off 4 sts, knit to end.
18[21,24,27,30] sts.

Next Row: P4, *k1, p1, k1, p5, rep from *
to last 6[9,4,7,2] sts, k1, p1, k1 [1,1,1,0],
p3[6,1,4,2].

Proceed as follows:

1st Row: Knit.

2nd Row: P4, *k1, p1, k1, p5, rep from *
to last 6[9,4,7,2] sts, k1, p1, k1 [1,1,1,0],
p3[6,1,4,2].

First and 2nd rows set pat. Keeping
continuity of pat as set throughout, cont
until armhole measures 2½[3,3½,3,3½]in
(6[8,9,8,9]cm), ending with a RS row.

SHAPE NECK

Next Row: Bind off 3[3,4,4,5] sts in pat,
pat to end. 15[18,20,23,25] sts.

Work 7 rows, dec one st at neck edge in
next and every foll alt row. 11[14,16,19,
21] sts. Cont without shaping until
armhole measures 4[4¾,5¼,5½,6]in (10[12,
13,14,15]cm), ending with a WS row.

SHAPE SHOULDER

Next Row: Bind off 5[7,8,9,10] sts in pat,
pat to end. 6[7,8,10,11] sts.

Next Row: Work in pat.

Bind off rem 6[7,8,10,11] sts in pat.

RIGHT FRONT

Work as given for Left Front to **.
22[25,28,31,34] sts.

1st and Every Alt Row: Knit.

2nd Row: P0[0,3,0,0], k0[1,1,0,1],
p2[4,4,2,4], *p4, k1, p4, rep from * to last
2 sts, p2.

4th Row: P0[0,2,0,0], k0[2,3,0,2], p2
[3,3,2,3], *p3, k3, p3, rep from * to last
2 sts, p2.

6th Row: P0[0,1,0,0], k0[3,5,0,3], p2, *p2,
k5, p2, rep from * to last 2 sts, p2.

8th Row: K0[4,7,0,4], p2[1,1,2,1], *p1, k7,
p1, rep from * to last 2 sts, p2.

10th Row: K0[0,3,0,0], p0[1,1,0,1],
k0[3,3,0,3], p2[1,1,2,1], *(p1, k3) twice,
p1, rep from * to last 2 sts, p2.

12th Row: (P1, k1, p1) 0[0,1,0,0] times,
p0[2,2,0,2], k0[1,1,0,1], p2, *p2, k1, p3,
k1, p2, rep from * to last 2 sts, p2.

Work 0[0,0,2,4] rows in St st.

Using A, work 3 rows in garter st.

Next Row: Using A, k10[12,14,16,18], m1,
(k1, m1) 3 times, k9[10,11,12,13].
26[29,32,35,38] sts.

Proceed as follows:

1st Row: K7[8,9,10,11]C; using A, p1,
C4B, C4F, p1; k9[11,13,15,17]C.

2nd Row: Using C, (k1, p1) 4[5,6,7,8] times, k1; k1A, p8A, k1A; p7[8,9,10,11]C.

3rd Row: K7[8,9,10,11]B; p1A, k8A, p1A; using C, k1, (p1, k1) 4[5,6,7,8] times.

4th Row: Using C, (p1, k1) 4[5,6,7,8] times, p1; k1A, p8A, k1A; p7[8,9,10,11]B.

5th Row: K7[8,9,10,11]C; using A, p1, C4F, C4B, p1; using C, (p1, k1) 4[5,6,7,8] times, p1.

First–5th rows set moss-st panel at side edge.

6th and 7th Rows: As 2nd and 3rd rows.

8th Row: Using C, (p1, k1) 4[5,6,7,8] times, p1; k1A, p8A, k1A; p7[8,9,10,11]B.

First–8th rows set cable panel and striped panel. Keeping continuity of pat panels, work 6[6,14,22,30] rows more.

Next Row: Using A, k8[9,10,11,12], (k2tog) 4 times, k10[12,14,16,18]. 22[25,28,31,34] sts.

Using A, work 3 rows in garter st. Using B

only throughout, proceed as follows:

Next Row: Knit.

SHAPE ARMHOLE

Next Row: Bind off 4 sts purlwise, p2[5,0,3,0], (k1, p5) 0[0,0,0,1] times, *k1, p1, k1, p5, rep from * to last 7 sts, k1, p1, k1, p4. 18[21,24,27,30] sts.

Proceed as follows:

1st Row: Knit.

2nd Row: P3[6,1,4,1], (k1, p5) 0[0,0, 0,1] times, *k1, p1, k1, p5, rep from * to last 7 sts, k1, p1, k1, p4.

First–2nd rows set pat. Keeping continuity of pat as set, cont until armhole measures 2½[3,3½,3,3½]in (6[8,9,8,9]cm), ending with a WS row.

SHAPE NECK

Next Row: Bind off 3[3,4,4,5] sts in pat, pat to end. 15[18,20,23,25] sts.

Work 8 rows, dec one st at neck edge in 2nd and every foll alt row. 11[14,16,19,21] sts.

Cont without shaping until armhole measures 4[4¾,5¼,5½,6]in (10[12,13,14, 15]cm), ending with a RS row.

SHAPE SHOULDER

Bind off 5[7,8,9,10] sts in pat at beg of next row. Work 1 row in pat.

Bind off rem 6[7,8,10,11] sts in pat.

SLEEVES

Using smaller needles and A, cast on 31[31,33,37,39] sts.

Work 7[7,7,9,9] rows in garter st.

Next Row: K5[4,4,5,5], (m1, k1) 4 times, k13[15,17,19,21], (m1, k1) 4 times, k5[4,4,5,5]. 39[39,41,45,47] sts.

Change to larger needles and proceed as follows:

1st Row: K4[3,3,4,4]C; using A, p1, C4B, C4F, p1; k11[13,15,17,19]C; using A, p1, C4B, C4F, p1; k4[3,3,4,4]C.

2nd Row: P4[3,3,4,4]C; k1A, p8A, k1A; using C, p1, (k1, p1) 5[6,7,8,9] times; k1A, p8A, k1A; p4[3,3,4,4]C.

techniques ▶

For increases   p. 22

For buttonholes   p. 43

3rd Row: Using B, k1, m1, k3[2,2,3,3]; p1A, k8A, p1A; using C, (p1, k1) 5[6,7,8,9] times, p1; p1A, k8A, p1A; using B, k3[2,2,3,3], m1, k1.

4th Row: P5[4,4,5,5]B; k1A, p8A, k1A; using C, k1, (p1, k1) 5[6,7,8,9] times; k1A, p8A, k1A; p5[4,4,5,5]B.

5th Row: K5[4,4,5,5]C; using A, p1, C4F, C4B, p1; using C, (k1, p1) 5[6,7,8,9] times, k1; using A, p1, C4F, C4B, p1; k5[4,4,5,5]C.

2nd to 5th rows center panel set moss st.

6th Row: Using C, (p1, m1) 0[1,1,0,0] times, p5[3,3,5,5]; k1A, p8A, k1A; using C, p1, (k1, p1) 5[6,7,8,9] times; k1A, p8A, k1A; using C, p5[3,3,5,5], (m1, p1) 0[1,1,0,0] times.

7th Row: Using B, (k1, m1) 1[0,0,1,1] times, k4[5,5,4,4]; p1A, k8A, p1A; using C, (p1, k1) 5[6,7,8,9] times, p1; p1A, k8A, p1A; using B, k4[5,5,4,4], (m1, k1) 1[0,0,1,1] times. 43[43,45,49,51] sts.

8th Row: P6[5,5,6,6]B; k1A, p8A, k1A; using C, k1, (p1, k1) 5[6,7,8,9] times; k1A, p8A, k1A; p6[5,5,6,6]B.

First–8th rows set cable panel and striped panels.

Keeping continuity of pat panels as set, inc 1 st at each end of 3rd[first,first, 3rd,3rd] and every foll 4th[3rd,3rd,4th,4th] row to 53[61,65,69,75] sts, working inc sts in striped pat.

Cont without shaping until sleeve measures 6½[7½,8¾,10¼,12]in (17[19,22, 26,31]cm), ending with a RS row.

Next Row: Pat 10[13,14,16,17]; using A, k1, (p2tog) 4 times, k1; pat 11[13,15,17, 19]C; using A, k1, (p2tog) 4 times, k1; pat 10[13,14,16,17]. 45[53,57,61,67] sts. Bind off in pat.

RIGHT FRONT BORDER

With RS facing and using smaller needles and A, pick up and knit 4[4,4,5,5] sts evenly along garter st and 36[40,49,58,69] sts evenly along front edge. 40[44,53,63, 74] sts. Work 2 rows in garter st.

For a Girl

Next Row: K3, bind off 2 sts, (k5[6,6,8,8], bind off 2 sts) 4[4,5,5,6] times, k2.

Next Row: K3, cast on 2 sts, (k6[7,7,9,9], cast on 2 sts) 4[4,5,5,6] times, k3.

Work 2 rows in garter st. Bind off.

For a Boy

Work 4 rows in garter st. Bind off.

LEFT FRONT BORDER

With RS facing and using smaller needles and A, pick up and knit 36[40,49,58,69] sts evenly along front edge and 4[4,4,5,5] sts evenly along garter st. 40[44,53,63,74] sts. Work 2 rows in garter st.

For a Girl

Work 4 rows in garter st. Bind off.

For a Boy

Next Row: K3, bind off 2 sts, (k5[6,6,8,8], bind off 2 sts) 4[4,5,5,6] times, k2.

Next Row: K3, cast on 2 sts, (k6[7,7,9,9], cast on 2 sts) 4[4,5,5,6] times, k3.

Work 2 rows in garter st. Bind off.

COLLAR

Join shoulder seams. With WS facing, using smaller needles and A, and starting at center of left front border, pick up and knit 2 sts along border; using C, pick up and knit 19[19,20,22,23] sts along left side of neck, 19[19,21,21,23] sts from back of neck, 19[19,20,22,23] sts along right side of neck; and using A, 2 sts along border, ending at center of right

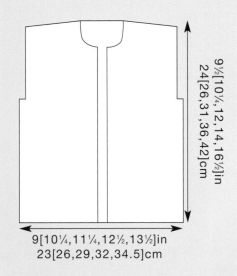

9½[10¼,12,14,16½]in
24[26,31,36,42]cm

9[10¼,11¼,12½,13½]in
23[26,29,32,34.5]cm

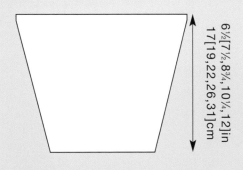

6½[7½,8¾,10¼,12]in
17[19,22,26,31]cm

front border. 61[61,65,69,73] sts.

Next Row: K2A; using C, k19[19,21,23, 19], inc in next st, (k5, inc in next st) 3[3,3, 3,5] times, k19[19,21,23,19]; k2A. 65[65, 69,73,79] sts.

Proceed as follows:

1st Row: K2A, *k1C, p1C, rep from * to last 3 sts, k1C, k2A.

2nd Row: K2A, p1C, *k1C, p1C, rep from * to last 2 sts, k2A.

3rd and 4th Rows: As 2nd and first rows. First–4th rows set pat.

Keeping continuity of pat as set, cont until collar measures 1½[1½,2,2,2½]in

(4[4,5,5,6]cm), ending with a RS row.

Next Row: K2A; using C, k20[20,22,24, 27], m1, (k4, m1) 5 times, k21[21,23,25, 28]; k2A. 71[71,75,79,85] sts.

Using A, work 3 rows in garter st. Bind off.

TO FINISH

Pin out garment to the measurements given at right. Cover with damp cloths and allow to dry. Join side seams. Join sleeve seams for 6[6½,8,9½,11½]in (15[17,20,24,29]cm). Sew sleeve top in position. Sew rest of sleeves to bound-off sts at armhole. Sew on buttons.

woman's beaded top

MAKE AN IMPACT AT
AN ELEGANT EVENING
OCCASION IN THIS
BEAUTIFUL BEADED
V-NECK TOP.
THE BEADS ARE
KNITTED RIGHT INTO
THE LUXURIOUS
CASHMERE FABRIC IN
A LATTICEWORK AND
DIAMOND PATTERN.

SKILL

3

ENJOY THE
CHALLENGE

woman's beaded top

Knitting with beads is easier than it looks. The background fabric is just plain stockinette stitch—follow a chart for the bead pattern. Beaded details on the hem, neck, and armhole borders give the top real designer class.

MEASUREMENTS

To fit Bust	in	32	34	36	38	40	42
	cm	81	86	91	97	102	107
Actual Size	in	34	36	38	40	42	44
	cm	88	92	98	102	108	112
Length	in	19½	19½	20	20½	21	21½
	cm	49	50	51	52	53	54

Figures in brackets [ ] refer to larger sizes; where there is only one set of figures, it applies to all sizes.

YOU WILL NEED

Number of 50g (1¾oz) skeins Jaeger Cashmina (shade 037):

	9	9	10	11	11	12

Pair of size 2 (2¾mm) knitting needles
Pair of size 3 (3¼mm) knitting needles
Approximately 3,700[3,900,4,100,4,300, 4,500,4,700] beads in first color (A)
Approximately 400[430,460,470,510,530] beads in second color (B)

GAUGE

28 sts and 36 rows to 4in (10cm) over St st on size 3 (3¼mm) needles or the size required to give the correct gauge.

ABBREVIATIONS

See page 95.

PATTERN NOTES

Before starting, thread beads onto yarn— see page 36 of techniques book. Since the first 20 chart rows are worked using two colors of beads, these need to be threaded onto the yarn in the reverse order to that needed for knitting. Reading chart (on page 52) from left to right, thread on beads required for 19th row, then still reading chart from left to right, thread on beads needed for 17th row. Continue in this way until beads for first chart row are on yarn. Now thread on 58[61,65,68, 72,75] more of bead A (for hem foldline row). Beads are now on skein of yarn in correct order for knitting up to end of 20th chart row. Once 20th chart row is completed, break yarn, thread on about 500 of bead A, rejoin yarn and continue following chart. To place a bead on RS (knit) rows, bring yarn to RS of work and slip a bead up next to stitch just worked. Slip next stitch purlwise, from left needle to right needle, and take yarn to WS of work, leaving bead sitting in front of slipped stitch. To place a bead on WS (knit foldline) rows, with yarn at back (RS) of work, slip a bead up next to stitch just worked. Keeping yarn at back (RS) of work, slip next stitch purlwise, from left needle to right needle, leaving bead sitting in front of slipped stitch.

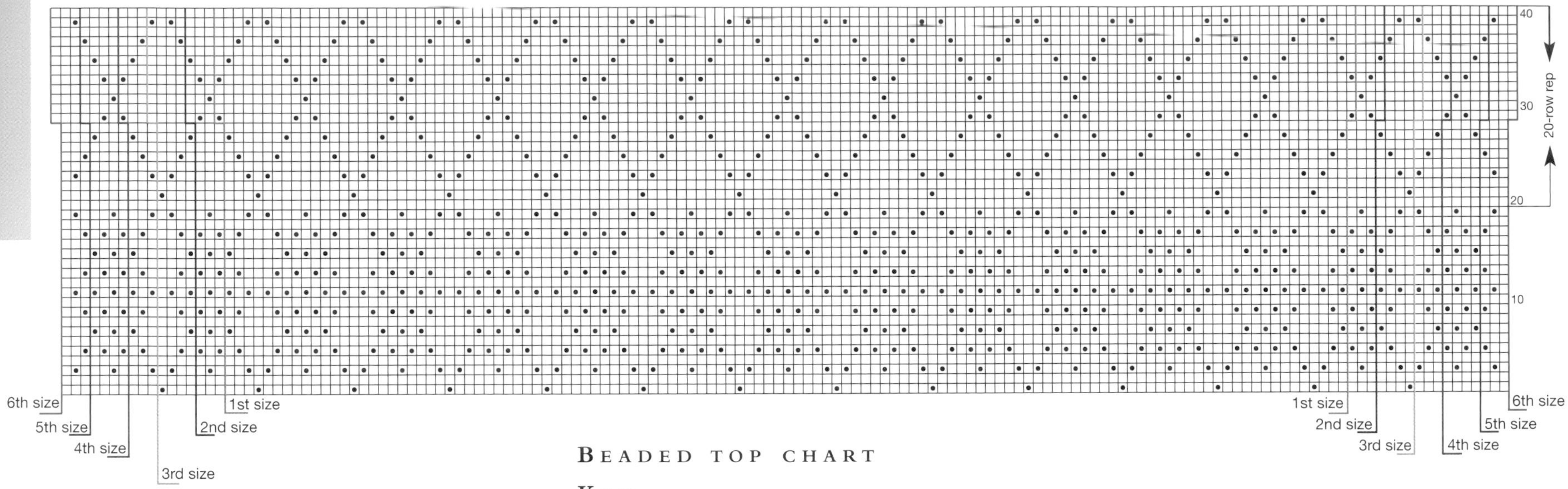

B E A D E D   T O P   C H A R T

K E Y

☐ = k on RS, p on WS

▪ = place bead A

▪ = place bead B

B A C K

Using smaller needles, cast on 117[123, 131,137,145,151] sts. Starting with a k

row, work in St st for 7 rows.

8th Row: (WS) K1, *place bead A, k1, rep from * to end (to form foldline). Change to larger needles. Starting with a k row, work in St st for 2 rows. Starting and ending rows as indicated, working first–20th rows once only, and then rep only 21st–40th rows as required, cont in pat, following chart in this way:

Work 24[24,24,28,28,28] rows, ending with RS facing for next row. Inc one st at each end of next and every foll 24th row until there are 123[129,137,143,151, 157] sts, working inc sts into pat. Cont without shaping until Back measures 12½[12½,12½,13,13,13½]in (31[32,32,33, 33,34]cm) from foldline row, ending with a WS row.

SHAPE ARMHOLES

Keeping pat correct, bind off 8[8,9,9, 10,10] sts at beg of next 2 rows. 107[113,119,125,131,137] sts. Dec 1 st at each end of next 3[5,5,7, 7,9] rows, then on foll 4[4,5,5,6,6] alt rows, then on every foll 4th row until 87[89, 93,95,99,101] sts rem. Cont even until armholes measure 7[7,7½,7½,8,8]in (18[18, 19,19,20,20]cm), ending with a WS row.

SHAPE SHOULDERS & BACK NECK

Bind off 8[8,8,8,9,9] sts at beg of next 2 rows. 71[73,77,79,81,83] sts.
Next Row: (RS) Bind off 8[8,8,8,9,9] sts, pat until there are 11[11,13,13,13,14] sts on right needle, turn and work this side first.
Bind off 4 sts at beg of next row.
Bind off rem 7[7,9,9,9,10] sts.
With RS facing, rejoin yarn to rem sts, bind off center 33[35,35,37,37,37] sts, pat to end. Work to match first side, reversing shapings.

FRONT

Work as given for Back until 20 rows less have been worked than on Back to start of armhole shaping, ending with a WS row.

DIVIDE FOR NECK

Next Row: (RS) Pat 60[63,67,70,74,77] sts, k2tog, turn and work this side first. Work 1 row. Keeping pat correct, dec 1 st at neck edge of next and foll 5[7,5,7,5,5] alt rows, then on foll 4th[0,4th,0,4th,4th] row. 54[56,61,63,68,71] sts. Work 3 rows even, ending with a WS row.

neck notes

After dividing the work for the V-neckline, each side of the neck is completed separately. While you are working the first side of the neck, leave the remaining stitches on a spare needle.

SHAPE ARMHOLE

Keeping pat correct, bind off 8[8,9,9,10, 10] sts at beg and dec 1 st at end of next row. 45 [47,51,53,57,60] sts. Work 1 row. Dec 1 st at armhole edge of next 3[5,5, 7,7,9] rows, then on foll 4[4,5,5,6,6] alt rows, then on 3 foll 4th rows and AT THE SAME TIME dec 1 st at neck edge of every foll 4th row from previous dec. 29[28,31,30,33,33] sts. Dec 1 st at neck edge only on every foll 4th row from previous dec until 23[23,25,25,27,28] sts rem. Cont even until Front matches Back to start of shoulder shaping, ending with a WS row.

SHAPE SHOULDER

Bind off 8[8,8,8,9,9] sts at beg of next and foll alt row. Work 1 row. Bind off rem 7[7,9,9,9,10] sts.
With RS facing, rejoin yarn to rem sts, pat to end. Work to match first side, reversing shapings and working an extra row before start of shoulder shaping.

techniques ▶

For decreases   p. 20

NECKBAND

Press carefully according to instructions on yarn label. Join right shoulder seam. Using bead A, thread 87[88,91,92,95,95] beads onto yarn. With RS facing and using smaller needles, pick up and knit 70[70,73,73,76,76] sts down left side of neck, one st from base of V (mark this st with a colored thread), 70[70,73,73,76, 76] sts up right side of neck, and 40[42, 42,44,44,44] sts from back neck. 181[183, 189,191,197,197] sts.

1st Row: (WS) P to within 1 st of marked st, p3tog (marked st is center st of this group), p to end.

2nd Row: K to within 1 st of marked st, sl1-k2tog-psso (marked st is center st of this group), k to end.

3rd Row: K1, *place bead A, k1, rep from * to end (to form foldline), working sl1-k2tog-psso over marked center front 3 sts. 175[177,183,185,191,191] sts.

4th Row: K to marked st, m1 (by picking up horizontal loop lying before next st and working into back of it), k marked st, m1, k to end.

5th Row: P to marked st, m1, p marked st, m1, p to end.

6th Row: As 4th row. 181[183,189,191,197,197]sts. Bind off purlwise (on WS), inc 1 st at either side of marked st as before.

ARMHOLE BORDERS

Join left shoulder and neck border seam. Fold neck border to inside along foldline and stitch in place.
Using bead A, thread 57[57,61,61,65,65] beads onto yarn. With RS facing and using smaller needles, pick up and knit 115[115,123,123,131,131] sts along one armhole. Starting with a p row, work in St st for 2 rows.

3rd Row: K1, *place bead, k1, rep from * to end (to form foldline).
Starting with a k row, work in St st for 3 rows. Bind off purlwise (on WS). Rep for remaining armhole.

MEASUREMENTS

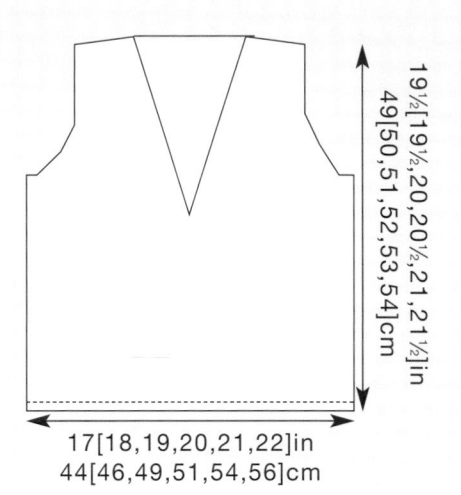

19½[19½,20,20½,21,21½]in
49[50,51,52,53,54]cm

17[18,19,20,21,22]in
44[46,49,51,54,56]cm

TO FINISH

Join side and armhole border seams. Fold armhole borders and first 7 rows around lower edge to inside along foldline and stitch in place.

techniques ▶

For sewing seams   p. 42

woman's jacket with loopy edging

SKILL

(2)

PRACTICE
MAKES
PERFECT

THIS FABULOUS
NATURAL, FLEECY
YARN WITH ITS
LOVELY TWEEDY
TEXTURE IS PERFECT
FOR A SIMPLE
STYLISH JACKET.
THE VERTICAL EDGES,
HEM, AND CUFFS ARE
COMPLEMENTED WITH
A FASHIONABLE
FLURRY OF THICK,
LOOPY CURLS.

woman's jacket with loopy edging   **project 11**

woman's jacket with loopy edging

The loopy trimming on this jacket resembles a curly fur fabric. Loop stitches are great fun and easier to work than you might think—just follow the instructions given in the pattern below.

MEASUREMENTS

To fit Bust						
	in	32	34	36	38	40
	cm	81	86	91	97	102
Actual Size	in	34	35½	38	40	43
	cm	86	90	97	101	109
Length	in	19½	20	20½	21	21½
	cm	50	51	52	53	54
Sleeve	in	17½	17½	17¾	17¾	17¾
	cm	44	44	45	45	45

Figures in brackets [ ] refer to larger sizes; where there is only one set of figures, it applies to all sizes.

YOU WILL NEED

Number of 3½oz (100g) skeins Jaeger Natural Fleece (shade 520):

7	8	8	9	9

Pair of size 13 (9mm) knitting needles
2 double-pointed size 13 (9mm) knitting needles

GAUGE

10½ sts and 15 rows to 4in (10cm) over St st on size 13 (9mm) needles or the size required to give the correct gauge.

ABBREVIATIONS

See page 95.

Make loop = K1 leaving st on left needle, bring yarn to front of work between needles, wrap it twice around thumb of left hand and take it back to WS of work between needles, k same st on left needle again and slip st off left needle, bring yarn to front of work between needles and take it back to WS of work by passing it over right needle, pass last 2 sts on right needle over this loop and off right needle—loop completed.

BACK

Using size 13 (9mm) needles, cast on 45[47, 51,53,57] sts. Work 2 rows in garter st. Work in pat as follows:
1st Row: (RS) K1, *make loop, k1, rep from * to end.
2nd Row: Knit.
3rd Row: K2, *make loop, k1, rep from * to last st, k1.
4th Row: Knit.
These 4 rows form pat.

easy texture

This yarn is so beautifully textured in itself that it knits up into an interesting fabric without the need for complicated stitch patterns. This is perfect for new knitters as mistakes are easily disguised.

Cont in pat, shaping side seams by dec one st at each end of 3rd and foll 6th row. 41[43,47,49,53] sts.
Work 1 row, ending with a WS row.
Beg with a k row, work in St st as follows:
Work 6 rows, ending with a WS row. Inc one st at each end of next and foll 12th row. 45[47,51,53,57] sts.

techniques ▶
For shaping   p. 20

Cont without shaping until Back measures 11½[12,12,12½,12½]in (30[31, 31,32,32]cm), ending with a WS row.

SHAPE ARMHOLES

Bind off 2[3,3,4,4] sts at beg of next 2 rows. 41[41,45,45,49] sts.

Next Row: (RS) K2, k2tog, k to last 4 sts, k2tog tbl, k2.

Next Row: P2, p2tog tbl, p to last 4 sts, p2tog, p2.

Working decreases as set, dec one st at each end of next 1[1,2,2,3] rows. 35[35, 37,37,39] sts. Cont without shaping until armholes measure 8[8,8½,8½,9]in (20[20, 21,21,22]cm), ending with a WS row.

SHAPE SHOULDERS & NECK

Next row: (RS) K2tog, k4[4,5,4,5], turn and complete this side first.

Bind off 3 sts at beg and dec one st at end of next row. Bind off rem 1[1,2,1,2] sts. With RS facing, rejoin yarn to rem sts, bind off center 23[23,23,25,25] sts, k to end. Complete to match first side, reversing shapings.

LEFT FRONT

Using size 13 (9mm) needles cast on 22[23,25,26,28] sts.

Work 2 rows in garter st.

Work in pat as follows:

1st Row: (RS) *K1, make loop, rep from * to last 2[1,1,2,2] sts, k2[1,1,2,2].

2nd Row: Knit.

3rd Row: K2, *make loop, k1, rep from * to last 0[1,1,0,0] sts, k0[1,1,0,0].

4th Row: Knit.

These 4 rows form pat.

Cont in pat, shaping side seam by dec one st at beg of 3rd and foll 6th row. 20[21,23,24,26] sts.

Next Row: (WS) K8, slip these sts onto a holder, M1, k to end. 13[14,16,17,19] sts. Beg with a k row, work in St st as follows: Work 6 rows, ending with a WS row. Inc one st at beg of next and foll 12th row. 15[16,18,19,21] sts.

Cont without shaping until Left Front matches Back to armholes, ending with a WS row.

SHAPE ARMHOLE

Bind off 2[3,3,4,4] sts at beg of next row. 13[13,15,15,17] sts.

Work 1 row.

SHAPE FRONT SLOPE

Next Row: (RS) K2, k2tog, k to last 4 sts, k2tog tbl, k2.

Next Row: P to last 4 sts, p2tog, p2. 10[10,12,12,14] sts.

Working all decreases as set by last 2 rows, dec one st at armhole edge of next 1[1,2,2,3] rows and AT THE SAME TIME dec 1[1,0,1,1] st at front slope of next row. 8[8,10,9,10] sts. Dec one st at front slope only of 4th[4th,next,next,2nd] and every foll 4th row until 3[3,4,3,4] sts rem.

Cont even until Left Front matches Back to shoulders, ending with a WS row.

SHAPE SHOULDER

Dec one st at armhole edge on next 2 rows. Bind off rem 1[1,2,1,2] sts.

RIGHT FRONT

Using size 13 (9mm) needles, cast on 22[23,25,26,28] sts. Work in garter st for 2 rows, ending with a WS row.

Work in pat as follows:
1st Row: (RS) K2[1,1,2,2], *make loop, k1, rep from * to end.
2nd Row: Knit.
3rd Row: K0[1,1,0,0], *k1, make loop, rep from * to last 2 sts, k2.
4th Row: Knit.

These 4 rows form pat.
Cont in pat, shaping side seam by dec one st at end of 3rd and foll 6th row. 20[21,23,24,26] sts.
Next Row: (WS) K to last 8 sts, M1 and turn, leaving last 8 sts on a holder. 13[14,16,17,19] sts.
Beg with a k row, work in St st as follows: Work 6 rows, ending with a WS row. Inc one st at end of next and foll 12th row. 15[16,18,19,21] sts.
Cont without shaping until Right Front matches Back to armholes, ending with a RS row.

going loopy

To practice making loops, knit a sample in garter stitch. Make loops on every other stitch in alternate rows, alternating their position in the row each time.

SHAPE ARMHOLE

Bind off 2[3,3,4,4] sts at beg of next row. 13[13,15,15,17] sts.

SHAPE FRONT SLOPE

Next Row: (RS) K2, k2tog, k to last 4 sts, k2tog tbl, k2.
Next Row: P2, p2tog tbl, p to end. 10[10,12,12,14] sts.
Complete to match Left Front, reversing

shapings, working an extra row before start of shoulder shaping.

SLEEVES

Using size 13 (9mm) needles, cast on 23[23,25,25,25] sts.
Work 2 rows in garter st.
Beg with a k row, work 4 rows in St st, ending with a WS row.
Work 10 rows in pat as given for Back, inc one st at each end of 5th of these rows and ending with a WS row. 25[25,27,27,27] sts.

Beg with a k row, cont in St st, shaping sides by inc one st at each end of 7th[3rd,3rd,next,next] and every foll

techniques ▶
For paired shapings p. 23

12th[10th,10th,8th,6th] row until there are 33[35,37,37,33] sts.

4th and 5th sizes only
Inc one st at each end of every foll [10th, 8th] row until there are [39,41] sts.

All sizes
Cont straight to 17½[17½,17¾,17¾,17¾]in (44[44,45,45,45]cm) or length required, ending with a WS row.

SHAPE SLEEVE TOP

Bind off 2[3,3,4,4] sts at beg of next 2 rows. 29[29,31,31,33] sts.
Working all decreases 2 sts in from ends of rows as before, dec 1 st at each end of next and every foll 4th row until 21[21,23,23,25] sts rem, then on every foll alt row until 17 sts rem, then on foll 3 rows, ending on WS. Bind off rem 11 sts.

LEFT FRONT BORDER

Join shoulder seams.
With RS of work facing, slip 8 sts left on Left Front holder onto size 13 (9mm) needles and rejoin yarn. Cont in pat until border, when slightly stretched, fits up left front opening edge, up front slope and across to center back neck, sewing into place as you go along, and ending with a WS row. Bind off.

RIGHT FRONT BORDER

With WS of work facing, slip 8 sts left on right front holder onto size 13 (9mm) needles and rejoin yarn. Complete to match Left Front Border.

TIES (MAKE 4)

Using size 13 (9mm) double-pointed needles, cast on 2 sts.
1st Row: (RS) K2, *without turning work slip these 2 sts to opposite end of needle and bring yarn to opposite end of work pulling it quite tightly across back of sts, using the other needle k these 2 sts again, rep from * until tie is 8in (20cm) long, then k2tog and fasten off.

TO FINISH

Press according to directions on yarn label. Join bound-off ends of borders at center back neck. Set in sleeves. Join side and sleeve seams. Attach 2 ties to front opening edges, sewing one tie to each front level with start of front slope shaping and 2 more ties 5in (13cm) below the first.

MEASUREMENTS

19½[20,20½,21,21½]in
50[51,52,53,54]cm

17[17¾,19,20,21½]in
43[45,48.5,50.5,54.5]cm

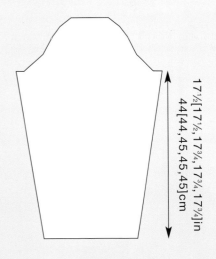

17½[17½,17¾,17¾,17¾]in
44[44,45,45,45]cm

girl's jacket with embroidery

SKILL

2

PRACTICE
MAKES
PERFECT

SHE'LL JUST LOVE THIS JACKET WITH ITS SIMPLE TEXTURED PATCHWORK AND PRETTY FLUTED EDGINGS. KNITTED IN A CREAM DENIM-STYLE YARN, IT'S LOVINGLY EMBROIDERED WITH BLUE HEARTS AND FLOWERS.

girl's jacket with embroidery   **project 12**

girl's jacket with embroidery

Adding embroidery afterward is an easy way to add pizzazz to a plain knitted garment. The patchwork background and naive appearance of the motifs give this jacket a Shaker-style simplicity.

MEASUREMENTS

To fit chest		22	24	26	28	30
	in	22	24	26	28	30
	cm	56	61	66	71	76
Actual Size	in	27	29	31	33	35
	cm	68	73	78	84	89
Length	in	11	12	13	14	15
	cm	28	31	33	36	38
Sleeve	in	9	10¾	12	13½	14½
	cm	23	27	31	34	37

Figures in brackets [ ] refer to larger sizes; where there is only one set of figures, it applies to all sizes.

YOU WILL NEED

Number of 1¾oz (50g) skeins Sirdar Denim Tweed DK (shade 502):

		3	4	4	6	6

Small amounts of shades 502 and 566 for embroidery
Pair size 6 (4mm) knitting needles
Pair size 5 (3¾mm) knitting needles
Size 5 (3¾mm) circular knitting needle, 32in (80cm) long
4[4,4,5,5] buttons

GAUGE

22 sts and 28 rows to 4in (10cm) over St st on size 6 (4mm) needles or the size required to give the correct gauge.

ABBREVIATIONS

See page 95.

easy patchwork

This jacket is knitted in a single color and divided into patches with lines of textured seed stitch.

LEFT FRONT

Using smaller needles, cast on 109[109, 119,119,129] sts.
1st Row: P1, *k7, p3, rep from * to last 8 sts, k7, p1.
2nd Row: K1, p7, *k3, p7, rep from * to last st, k1.
3rd Row: P1, *sl1-k1-psso, k3, k2tog, p3, rep from * to last 8 sts, sl1-k1-psso, k3, k2tog, p1.

4th Row: K1, p5, *k3, p5, rep from * to last st, k1.
5th Row: P1, *sl1-k1-psso, k1, k2tog, p3, rep from * to last 6 sts, sl1-k1-psso, k1, k2tog, p1.
6th Row: K1, p3, *k3, p3, rep from * to last st, k1.
7th Row: P1, *sl1-k2tog-psso, p3, rep from * to last 4 sts, sl1-k2tog-psso, p1. 43[43,47,47,51] sts.
8th Row: Pat and slip 6 sts onto a stitch holder, pat to end, dec 2[0,1,0,0] sts evenly across row for first and 3rd sizes only and inc 0[0,0,2,1] sts evenly across row for 4th and 5th sizes only. 35[37,40,43,46] sts.
Change to larger needles.
Proceed as follows:
**1st Row: P1[1,0,1,0], *k1, p1, rep from * to end.

2nd Row: *P1, k1, rep from * to last 1[1,0,1,0] sts, p1[1,0,1,0].

3rd and 4th Rows: As first and 2nd rows.

5th Row: K0[2,5,8,11], p1, k1, p1, k15, p1, k1, p1, k14.

6th Row: P15, k1, p17, k1, p1[3,6,9,12].

7th-26th Rows: Rep 5th and 6th rows 10 times more.**

From ** to ** sets the pat. Keeping pat correct throughout, cont until left front measures 9[10¼,11,12,12½]in (23[26,28, 30,32]cm), ending with a RS row.

matching the pattern

If you are working in pattern, before shaping the armholes, make sure that you finish with the same pattern row on the fronts and back of the garment.

SHAPE NECK

Next Row: Bind off 4[5,6,6,7] sts in pat, pat to end.

Work 5 rows, dec one st at neck edge on every row. 26[27,29,32,34] sts. Cont without shaping until left front measures 11[12,13,14,15]in (28[31,33, 36,38]cm), ending with a WS row. Bind off in pat.

RIGHT FRONT

Using smaller needles, cast on 109[109, 119,119,129] sts.

1st Row: P1, *k7, p3, rep from * to last 8 sts, k7, p1.

2nd Row: K1, p7, *k3, p7, rep from * to last st, k1.

3rd Row: P1, *sl1-k1-psso, k3, k2tog, p3, rep from * to last 8 sts, sl1-k1-psso, k3, k2tog, p1.

4th Row: K1, p5, *k3, p5, rep from * to last st, k1.

5th Row: P1, *sl1-k1-psso, k1, k2tog, p3, rep from * to last 6 sts, sl1-k1-psso, k1, k2tog, p1.

6th Row: K1, p3, *k3, p3, rep from * to last st, k1.

7th Row: P1, *sl1-k2tog-psso, p3, rep from * to last 4 sts, sl1-k2tog-psso, p1. 43[43,47,47,51] sts.

8th Row: Pat to last 6 sts, dec 2[0,1,0, 0] sts evenly across row for first and 3rd sizes only and inc 0[0,0,2,1] sts evenly across row for 4th and 5th sizes only, slip rem 6 sts onto a stitch holder. 35[37,40,43,46] sts.

Change to larger needles.

Proceed as follows:

**1st Row: *P1, k1, rep from * to last 1[1,0,1,0] sts, p1[1,0,1,0] sts.

2nd Row: P1[1,0,1,0], *k1, p1, rep from * to end.

3rd and 4th Rows: As first and 2nd rows.

5th Row: K14, p1, k1, p1, k15, p1, k1, p1, k0[2,5,8,11].

6th Row: P1[3,6,9,12], k1, p17, k1, p15.

7th-26th Rows: Rep 5th and 6th rows 10 times more.**

Keeping pat correct throughout, cont until right front measures 9[10¼,11,12, 12½]in (23[26,28,30,32]cm), ending with a WS row.

SHAPE NECK

Next Row: Bind off 4[5,6,6,7] sts in pat, pat to end.

Next Row: Work in pat to end.

Work 5 rows, dec one st at neck edge on every row. 26[27,29,32,34] sts. Cont without shaping until right front measures 11[12,13,14,15]in (28[31,33, 36, 38]cm), ending with a WS row. Bind off in pat.

BACK

Using smaller needles, cast on 189[199, 219,229,249] sts.

1st Row: P1, *k7, p3, rep from * to last 8 sts, k7, p1.

2nd Row: K1, p7, *k3, p7, rep from * to last st, k1.

3rd Row: P1, *sl1-k1-psso, k3, k2tog, p3, rep from * to last 8 sts, sl1-k1-psso, k3, k2tog, p1.

4th Row: K1, p5, *k3, p5, rep from * to last st, k1.

5th Row: P1, *sl1-k1-psso, k1, k2tog, p3, rep from * to last 6 sts, sl1-k1-psso, k1, k2tog, p1.

6th Row: K1, p3, *k3, p3, rep from * to last st, k1.

7th Row: K1, *sl1-k2tog-psso, p3, rep from * to last 4 sts, sl1-k2tog-psso, k1. 75[79,87,91,99] sts.

8th Row: Pat to end, dec 0[0,2,0,2] sts evenly across row. 75[79,85,91,97] sts. Change to larger needles.

Proceed as follows:

**1st Row: P1[1,0,1,0], *k1, p1, rep from * to last 0[0,1,0,1] sts, k0[0,1,0,1].

2nd–4th Rows: Rep first row 3 times more.

5th Row: K0[2,5,8,11], (p1, k1, p1, k15) 4 times, p1, k1, p1, k0[2,5,8,11].

6th Row: P1[3,6,9,12], k1, p1, (p16, k1, p1) 4 times, p0[2,5,8,11].

7th–26th Rows: Rep 5th and 6th rows 10 times more.**

From ** to ** sets pat. Keeping pat correct throughout, cont until back measures 11[12,13,14,15]in (28[31,33, 36,38]cm), ending with a WS row.
Bind off in pat.

SLEEVES

Using smaller needles, cast on 119[119, 129,139,139] sts.

1st Row: P1, *k7, p3, rep from * to last 8 sts, k7, p1.

2nd Row: K1, p7, *k3, p7, rep from * to last st, k1.

3rd Row: P1, *sl1-k1-psso, k3, k2tog, p3, rep from * to last 8 sts, sl1-k1-psso, k3, k2tog, p1.

4th Row: K1, p5, *k3, p5, rep from * to last st, k1.

5th Row: P1, *sl1-k1-psso, k1, k2tog, p3, rep from * to last 6 sts, sl1-k1-psso, k1, k2tog, p1.

6th Row: K1, p3, *k3, p3, rep from * to last st, k1.

7th Row: P1, *sl1-k2tog-psso, p3, rep from * to last 4 sts, sl1-k2tog-psso, p1. 47[47,51,55,55] sts.

8th Row: Pat to end, inc 0[0,2,2,2] sts evenly across row. 47[47,53,57,57] sts. Change to larger needles.

Proceed as follows:

1st Row: P1[1,0,0,0], *k1, p1, rep from * to last 0[0,1,1,1] sts, k0[0,1,1,1].

2nd–4th Rows: Rep first row 3 times more.

5th Row: K4[4,7,9,9], (p1, k1, p1, k15) twice, p1, k1, p1, k4[4,7,9,9].

6th Row: P5[5,8,10,10], k1, p1, (p16, k1, p1) twice, p4[4,7,9,9].

7th and 8th Rows: As 5th and 6th rows.

techniques ▶

For paired shapings p. 23

9th Row: K1, m1, k3[3,6,8,8], (p1, k1, p1, k15) twice, p1, k1, p1, k3[3,6,8,8], m1, k1.

10th Row: P6[6,9,11,11], k1, p1, (p16, k1, p1) twice, p5[5,8,10,10].

11th Row: K5[5,8,10,10], (p1, k1, p1, k15) twice, p1, k1, p1, k5[5,8,10,10].

12th Row: As 10th row.

13th Row: (K1, m1) 1[1,0,0,0] times, k4[4,8,10,10], (p1, k1, p1, k15) twice, p1, k1, p1, k4[4,8,10,10], (m1, k1) 1[1,0,0,0] times.

14th Row: (P1, m1) 0[0,1,1,1] times, p7[7,8,10,10], k1, p1, (p16, k1, p1) twice, p6[6,7,9,9], (m1, p1) 0[0,1, 1,1] times.

15th Row: K6[6,9,11,11], (p1, k1, p1, k15) twice, p1, k1, p1, k6[6,9,11,11].

16th Row: P7[7,10,12,12], k1, p1, (p16, k1, p1) twice, p6[6,9,11,11].

17th Row: (K1, m1) 1[1,0,0,0] times, k5[5,9,11,11], (p1, k1, p1, k15) twice, p1, k1, p1, k5[5,9,11,11], (m1, k1) 1[1,0,0,0] times.

18th Row: P8[8,10,12,12], k1, p1, (p16, k1, p1) twice, p7[7,9,11,11].

19th Row: (K1, m1) 0[0,1,1,1] times, k7[7,8,10,10], (p1, k1, p1, k15) twice, p1, k1, p1, k7[7,8,10,10], (m1, k1) 0[0,1,1,1] times.

20th Row: P8[8,11,13,13], k1, p1, (p16, k1, p1) twice, p7[7,10,12,12].

21st Row: (K1, m1) 1[1,0,0,0] times, k6[6,10,12,12], (p1, k1, p1, k15) twice, p1, k1, p1, k6[6,10,12,12], (m1, k1) 1[1,0,0,0]

times.

22nd Row: P9[9,11,13,13], k1, p1, (p16, k1, p1) twice, p8[8,10,12,12].

23rd Row: K8[8,10,12,12], (p1, k1, p1, k15) twice, p1, k1, p1, k8[8,10,12,12].

24th Row: (P1, m1) 0[0,1,1,1] times, p9[9,10,12,12], k1, p1, (p16, k1, p1) twice, p8[8,9,11,11], (m1, p1) 0[0,1,1,1] times.

25th Row: (K1, m1) 1[1,0,0,0] times, k7[7,11,13,13], (p1, k1, p1, k15) twice, p1, k1, p1, k7[7,11,13,13], (m1, k1) 1[1,0,0,0] times. 57[57,61,65,65] sts.

26th Row: P10[10,12,14,14], k1, p1, (p16, k1, p1) twice , p9[9,11,13,13].

First–26th rows set pat.

Keeping pat correct and inc as set, cont to 67[73,77,83,89] sts, working inc sts in pat.

Cont even until sleeve measures 9[10¾, 12,13½,14½]in (23[27,31,34,37]cm), ending with a WS row. Bind off in pat.

RIGHT FRONT BORDER

Using smaller needles and with WS facing, cast on 1 st (this st to be used for sewing front border in place), work across 6 sts left on a stitch holder as follows: (p1, k1) 3 times.

1st Row: (K1, p1) 3 times.

Rep first row 3 times more.

**Next Row: K1, p1, bind off 2 sts, p1, k1.

Next Row: K1, p1, k1, cast on 2 sts,

p1, k1.

Rep first row 22[24,26,22,24] times more.**

Work from ** to ** 2[2,2,3,3] times more.

Next Row: K1, p1, bind off 2 sts, p1, k1.

Next Row: K1, p1, k1, cast on 2 sts, p1, k1.

Rep first row 4 times more. Bind off.

LEFT FRONT BORDER

Using smaller needles and with RS facing, cast on one st (this st to be used for sewing front border in place), work across 6 sts left on a stitch holder as follows: (p1, k1) 3 times.

1st Row: (K1, p1) 3 times.

Rep first row 80[86,92,104,112] times more. Bind off in seed st.

COLLAR

Join shoulder seams.
Using smaller needles and with RS facing, commencing at center of right front border pick up and knit 25[26,27, 30,31] sts evenly along right side of neck, 23[25,27,27,29] sts from back of neck, and 25[26,27,30,31] sts evenly along left side of neck, ending at center of left front border. 73[77,81,87,91] sts.
Work in seed st for 2¼[2¼,2¼,3¼,3¼]in (6[6,6,8,8]cm), ending with a WS row.
Bind off in seed st.

COLLAR EDGING

Using smaller needles or circular needle, cast on 189[199,209,219,239] sts.

1st Row: P1, *k7, p3, rep from * to last 8 sts, k7, p1.
2nd Row: K1, p7, *k3, p7, rep from * to last st, k1.
3rd Row: P1, *sl1-k1-psso, k3, k2tog, p3, rep from * to last 8 sts, sl1-k1-psso, k3, k2tog, p1.
4th Row: K1, p5, *k3, p5, rep from * to last st, k1.
5th Row: P1, *sl1-k1-psso, k1, k2tog, p3, rep from * to last 6 sts, sl1-k1-psso, k1, k2tog, p1.
6th Row: K1, p3, *k3, p3, rep from * to last st, k1.
7th Row: P1, *sl1-k2tog-psso, p3, rep from * to last 4 sts, sl1-k2tog-psso, p1. 75[79,83,87,95] sts. Bind off in pat.

TO FINISH

Press according to directions on yarn label. Work duplicate stitch and embroidery following the instructions given with the chart—see below.
Fold sleeves in half lengthwise, then placing folds to shoulder seams, sew sleeves in position. Join side and sleeve seams. Sew front borders in position (using cast-on sts). Sew collar edging evenly in position along edge of collar. Sew on buttons.

DUPLICATE STITCH CHART KEY

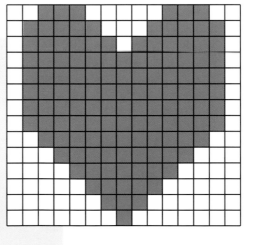

■ = duplicate stitch worked over 1 stitch and 1 row. For more details on working duplicate stitch, see the techniques book, page 38.

Using remnants of blue denim yarn, work duplicate stitch on squares as required for heart motif from chart. Using straight stitch, work vertical and horizontal lines on top of the motif.
Embroider other squares as required for flowers worked in lazy daisy stitch. For more details on working lazy daisy stitch, see the techniques book, page 39.

MEASUREMENTS

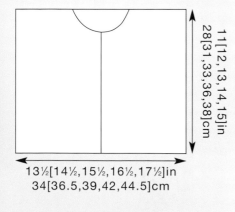

11[12,13,14,15]in
28[31,33,36,38]cm

13½[14½,15½,16½,17½]in
34[36.5,39,42,44.5]cm

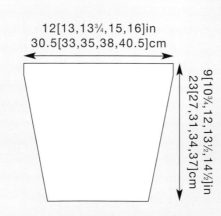

12[13,13¾,15,16]in
30.5[33,35,38,40.5]cm

9[10¾,12,13½,14½]in
23[27,31,34,37]cm

colorful collection

Have fun with projects in color patterns featuring a range of techniques—stripes, patchwork, intarsia, and Fair Isle. Brighten up a child's day with a cheerful hat. Cover a baby in a pretty patchwork blanket. Make traditional Fair Isle vests. And greet the sun in a zingy summer top.

child's hat
and scarf set

child's hat and scarf set

SKILL

2

PRACTICE
MAKES
PERFECT

THIS CHEERFUL HAT
AND SCARF SET,
FEATURING A JOLLY
RED HEART MOTIF, IS
ESSENTIAL OUTDOOR
GEAR FOR COLD
WINTER WINDS.
THERE'S A CHOICE OF
HAT STYLES FOR BOYS
OR GIRLS AND THE
SCARF IS TRIMMED
WITH A POMPON.

child's hat and scarf set   **project 13**

child's hat and scarf set

Working the striped background of this hat and scarf is easy with an ingenious novelty yarn that forms stripes as you are working. The heart motifs and border design are worked in intarsia and Fair Isle techniques.

MEASUREMENTS

To fit Years	1-2	3-4	5-6

Figures in brackets [ ] refer to larger sizes; where there is only one set of figures, it applies to all sizes.

YOU WILL NEED

Number of 1¾oz (50g) skeins Sirdar Snuggly Magic DK:

Hat with ear flaps

A (main color—shade180)	1	1	1
B (contrast—shade 242)	1	1	1

Beret

A (main color—shade 180)	1	1	1
B (contrast—shade 242)	1	1	1

Scarf

A (main color—shade180)	2
B (contrast—shade 242)	1

Pair of size 3 (3¼mm) knitting needles
Pair of size 6 (4mm) knitting needles

GAUGE

22 sts and 28 rows to 4in (10cm) over St st on size 6 (4mm) needles or the size required to give the correct gauge.

ABBREVIATIONS

See page 95.

HAT WITH EAR FLAPS

EAR FLAPS (BOTH ALIKE)

Using larger needles and A, cast on 7[9,11] sts. Purl 1 row.
Cont in St st, beg with a knit row, and AT THE SAME TIME inc one st at each end of the next 4 rows, then on the 4 foll alt rows. 23[25,27] sts.
Work 2 rows, then work first–5th rows from Chart 1, placing pat as follows:
1st Row: K0[1,2]B, k1A, *k2A, k2B, k1A, rep from * to last 2[3,4] sts, k2A, k0[1,2]B.
Work 5 rows more in A, ending with a WS row.
Cut off yarn and leave sts on a spare needle.

CHART 1

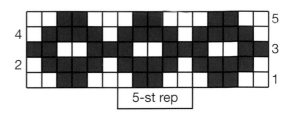

5-st rep

KEY

☐ = A
■ = B

MAIN BODY OF HAT

Using larger needles and A, cast on 96[104,112] sts.
Cont in St st, beg with a knit row, and work 14 rows.

POSITION EAR FLAPS

Next Row: K11[12,13], then work across 23[25,27] sts from one ear flap tog with sts from main body as follows: with flap sts behind hat sts, knit next st with first st from one ear flap tog and slip both sts from needles, cont in this way until all sts from ear flap have been worked, knit the next 28[30,32] sts from main body of hat, then work sts from second ear flap as given for first, knit rem 11[12,13] sts.
Work 7 rows more in A.

CHART 2

```
14  .  ■  ■  .  .  ■  ■  .
        ■  ■  .  .  ■  ■         13
12  ■  ■  ■  .  .  ■  ■  ■
    ■  ■  ■  ■  .  ■  ■  ■       11
10  ■  ■  ■  ■  ■  ■  ■  ■
    ■  ■  ■  ■  ■  ■  ■  ■        9
8   ■  ■  ■  ■  ■  ■  ■  ■
    ■  ■  ■  ■  ■  ■  ■  ■         7
6   .  ■  ■  ■  ■  ■  ■  .
    .  ■  ■  ■  ■  ■  ■  .         5
4   .  .  ■  ■  ■  ■  .  .
    .  .  ■  ■  ■  ■  .  .         3
2   .  .  .  ■  ■  .  .  .
    .  .  .  .  .  .  .  .         1
```

KEY

□ = A   ■ = B

Cont to work from Chart 2, placing heart as follows:

1st Row: (RS) K7[9,11]A, *k1B for heart, k15[16,17]A, rep from * to last 9[10, 11] sts, k1B for heart, k8[9,10]A.

2nd Row: P7[8,9]A, *p3B for heart, p13[14,15]A, rep from * to last 9[11, 13] sts, p3B for heart, p6[8,10]A.

Cont until all 14 rows have been worked. Work 4 rows in A. Then work 1st-5th rows from Chart 1, placing pat as follows:

1st Row: K0[1,1]A, *k2A, k2B, k1A, rep from * to last 1[3,1] sts, k1[2,1]A, k0[1,0]B.

Work 4 rows in A, 2 rows in B, 1 row in A. Cont in A only.

SHAPE CROWN

1st Row: K1, *k2tog, k6, rep from * to last 7 sts, k2tog, k5. 84[91,98] sts.

2nd and Every Alt Row: Purl.

3rd Row: K1, *k2tog, k5, rep from * to last 6 sts, k2tog, k4. 72[78,84] sts.

5th Row: K1, *k2tog, k4, rep from * to last 5 sts, k2tog, k3. 60[65,70] sts.

7th Row: K1, *k2tog, k3, rep from * to last 4 sts, k2tog, k2. 48[52,56] sts.

9th Row: K1, *k2tog, k2, rep from * to last 3 sts, k2tog, k1. 36[39,42] sts.

11th Row: K1, *k2tog, k1, rep from * to last 2 sts, k2tog. 24[26,28] sts.

12th Row: *K2tog, rep from * to end. 12[13,14] sts.

Cut off yarn and thread end through all the sts, pull up tightly and secure.

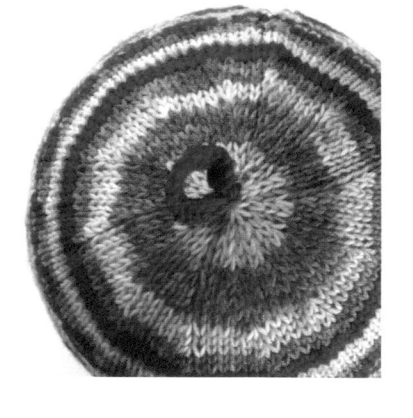

EAR FLAP EDGINGS

Join back seam, reversing it on last 14 rows for brim.

Using larger needles, RS facing and B, pick up and knit 56 sts around ear flap.

Next Row: Knit.

Bind off loosely.

CORDS (WORK 2)

Using larger needles and B, cast on 44 sts.

Next Row: Bind off 44 sts.

Attach one cord to center of each ear flap.

techniques ▶

For stranded color knitting   p. 32-33

LOOP

Using larger needles and B, cast on
16 sts.
Next Row: Bind off 16 sts.
Fold loop in half and attach to center
of crown.

BERET

With smaller needles and B, cast on
95[103,111] sts.
1st Row: (RS) *K1, p1, rep from * to last
st, k1.
2nd Row: With A, *p1, k1, rep from * to
last st, p1.
3rd Row: *K1, p1, rep from * to last st, k1.
Rep the last 2 rows until work measures
1in (3cm) from beg, ending with a RS row.
Inc Row: (WS) *Rib 2, m1, rib 3, m1, rib 2,
m1, rep from * 12[12,13] times more, (m1,
rib 2[3,4]) 2[3,2] times in all, m0[1,1], rib
0[3,5]. 136[146,156] sts.
Change to larger needles. Cont in St st,
beg with a knit row. Work 8 rows, then
work 5 rows from Chart 1, placing pat as
follows:
1st Row: *K2A, k2B, k1A, rep from
* to last st, k1A.
Cont in A, work 9 rows St st.

SHAPE CROWN

1st Row: (RS) *K13[14,15]A, k1B,
k13[14,15]A, rep from * ending with
k14[15,16]A.
2nd Row: P13[14,15]A, *p3B, p24[26,28]A,
rep from * ending with p12[13,14]A.
3rd Row: (dec row) *K3tog, k8[9,10]A,
k5B, k8[9,10]A, k3tog tblA, rep from * to
last st, k1A. 116[126,136] sts.
4th Row: P9[10,11]A, *p7B, p16[18,20]A,
rep from * ending with p8[9,10]A.
5th Row: K7[8,9]A, *k9B, k14[16,18]A, rep
from * ending with k8[9,10]A.
6th Row: P7[8,9]A, *p11B, p12[14,16]A,
rep from * ending with p6[7,8]A.
7th Row: K5[6,7]A, *k13B, k10[12,14]A,
rep from * ending with k6[7,8]A.
8th Row: P6[7,8]A, *p13B, p10[12,14]A,
rep from * ending with p5[6,7]A.
9th Row: (dec row) *K3togA, k2[3,4]A,
k13B, k2[3,4]A, k3tog tblA, rep from * to
last st, k1A. 96[106,116] sts.
10th Row: P4[5,6]A, *p13B, p6[8,10]A, rep
from * ending with p3[4,5]A.
11th Row: K3[4,5]A, *k13B, k6[8,10]A, rep
from * ending with k4[5,6]A.
12th Row: P4[5,6]A, *p6B, p1A, p6B,
p6[8,10]A, rep from * ending with
p3[4,5]A.
13th Row: K3[4,5]A, *k6B, k1A, k6B,
k6[8,10]A, rep from * ending with k4[5,6]A.
14th Row: P5[6,7]A, *p4B, p3A, p4B,
p8[10,12]A, rep from * ending with
p4[5,6]A.

15th Row: (dec row) *K3togA, k2[3,4]A,
k2B, k5A, k2B, k2[3,4]A, k3tog tblA, rep
from * to last st, k1A. 76[86,96] sts.
16th Row: With A, purl.
17th Row: With A, knit.
18th Row: With B, purl.
19th Row: With B, knit.

20th Row: With A, purl.
21st Row: With A, *k3tog, k9[11,13], k3tog tbl, rep from * to last st, k1. 56[66,76] sts.
22nd, 24th, and 26th Rows: With A, purl.
23rd Row: (dec row) *K3tog, k5[7,9], k3tog tbl, rep from * to last st, k1. 36[46,56] sts.
25th Row: (dec row) *K3tog, k1[3,5], k3tog tbl, rep from * to last st, k1. 16[26,36] sts.
27th Row: (dec row) K2tog all across row. 8[13,18] sts.

3rd size only
28th Row: Purl.
29th Row: K2tog all across row. 9 sts.

All sizes
Cut off yarn and thread end through rem sts, pull up tightly and secure.

TO FINISH

Join seam. Make loop as given for Hat with Ear Flaps and attach to center of crown.

perfect pompons

Cut two 2in (5cm) cardboard circles with a large central hole. With the circles together, wind yarn around the outer ring. Separate circles, cut outer edge of yarn between circles, and bind securely around center. Remove cardboard and trim pompon.

SCARF

Using larger needles and A, cast on 67 sts. Cont in St st, beg with a knit row. Work 8 rows in A, 2 rows in B, 4 rows in A, now work the 5 rows from Chart 1, placing pat as follows:
Next Row: K1A, *k2A, k2B, k1A, rep from * 12 times more, k1A.
Work 4 rows in A, 2 rows in B, 5 rows in A, then work from Chart 2, placing heart as follows:
Next Row: K9A, *k1B for heart, k15A, rep from * to last 10 sts, k1B for heart, k9A.
Work 4 rows in A, 2 rows in B, 4 rows in A, then work the 5 rows from Chart 1 as before, work 4 rows in A, 2 rows in B. Cont in A, work 15¾[16½,17¼]in (40[42, 44]cm) in St st, ending with a p row. Turn Charts upside down. Now reading charts from left to right on k rows and from right to left on p rows and working rows in reverse order, work the 65 rows in pat as for first side. Bind off.

TO FINISH

Fold scarf in half lengthwise and join the long seam. Gather short ends, pull up and secure. With B, make 2 pompons and attach one to each end.

child's intarsia sweater

DRESS UP A YOUNGSTER'S DENIM JEANS WITH THIS CHEERY, BRIGHT SWEATER. STYLIZED FLORAL MOTIFS ACROSS THE CHEST AND BROAD STRIPES ON THE SLEEVES MAKE AN UNUSUAL COMBINATION THAT LOOKS FRESH AND FASHIONABLE.

child's intarsia sweater   **project 14**

child's intarsia sweater

Although this sweater is entirely in stockinette stitch, with garter-stitch edgings, the flowers are formed with the intarsia technique. In this form of color knitting, separate skeins of yarn are used for each area of color.

MEASUREMENTS

To fit Chest	in	26	28	30	32
	cm	66	71	76	81
Actual Size	in	33	35	37	40
	cm	83	89	95	101
Length	in	18	19	20½	21½
	cm	46	49	52	55
Sleeve	in	16	17	18½	19½
	cm	41	43	47	49

Figures in brackets [ ] refer to larger sizes; where there is only one set of figures, it applies to all sizes.

YOU WILL NEED

Number of 1¾oz (50g) skeins Rowan Handknit DK Cotton:

A (shade 306)	6	7	8	9
B (shade 305)	2	3	3	3
C (shade 202)	2	2	2	2
D (shade 307)	3	3	3	4

Pair of size 6 (4mm) knitting needles
Pair of size 3 (3¼mm) knitting needles

GAUGE

20 sts and 28 rows to 4in (10cm) over St st on size 6 (4mm) needles or the size required to give the correct gauge.

ABBREVIATIONS

See page 95.

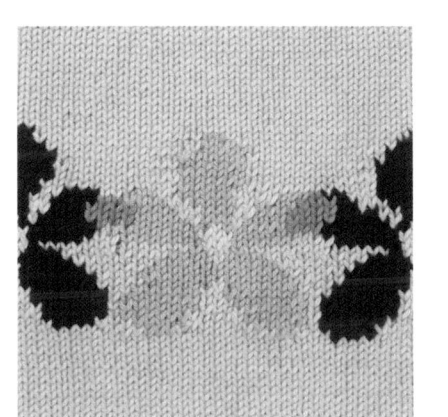

BACK

Using smaller needles and yarn B, cast on 83[89,95,101] sts.
Work in garter st (knit every row) for 8 rows, ending with a WS row.

Break off yarn B and join in yarn A.
Change to larger needles.
Beg with a k row, work in St st until back measures 9½[10,10½,11]in (25[26,27,28]cm), ending with a WS row.

PLACE FLOWER CHART

Using the intarsia technique (see technique book, page 31 for more details), starting and ending rows as indicated, and working in St st in pat foll chart on page 75, work 6 rows, ending with a WS row.

SHAPE ARMHOLES

Keeping chart correct, bind off 5 sts at beg of next 2 rows. 73[79,85,91] sts. Work 19 rows more to complete flower chart.

Break off contrast yarns. Using yarn A only, cont without shaping until armholes measure 7[8,8½,9½]in (18[20,22,24]cm), ending with a WS row.

techniques ▶

For intarsia	p. 31
For gauge	p. 45

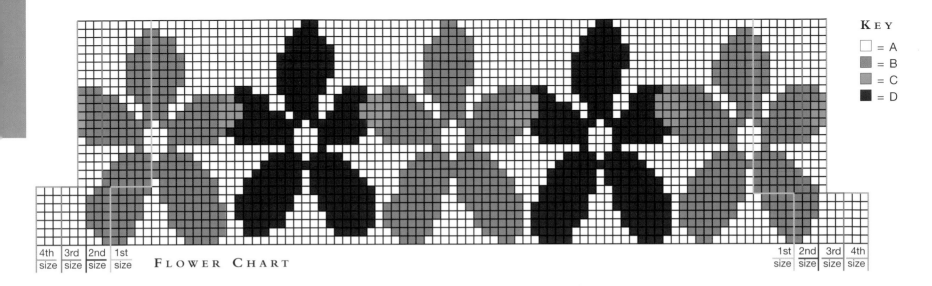

KEY

☐ = A
▨ = B
▩ = C
◼ = D

FLOWER CHART

| 4th size | 3rd size | 2nd size | 1st size | | 1st size | 2nd size | 3rd size | 4th size |

SHAPE SHOULDERS & NECK

Bind off 6[7,8,8] sts at beg of next
2 rows. 61[65,69,75] sts.

Next Row: (RS) Bind off 6[7,8,8] sts, k
until there are 11[11,11,13] sts on right
needle and turn, leaving rem sts on a
stitch holder for second side.
Work each side of neck separately.
Bind off 4 sts at beg of next row.
Bind off rem 7[7,7,9] sts.
With RS facing, rejoin yarn to rem sts,
bind off center 27[29,31,33] sts, k to end.
Complete to match first side of neck,
reversing shapings.

FRONT

Work as given for Back until 8[8,8,10]
rows less have been worked than on back
to start of shoulder shaping, ending with
a WS row.

SHAPE FRONT NECK

Next Row: (RS) K24[26,28,31] sts and
turn, leaving rem sts on a stitch holder.
Work each side of neck separately. Dec
one st at neck edge of next 4 rows, then
on foll 1[1,1,2] alt rows. 19[21,23,25] sts.
Work 1 row, ending with a WS row.

SHAPE SHOULDER

Bind off 6[7,8,8] sts at beg of next and
foll alt row. Work 1 row.
Bind off rem 7[7,7,9] sts.
   With RS facing, rejoin yarn to rem sts,
bind off center 25[27,29,29] sts, k to end.
Complete to match first side of neck,
reversing shapings.

techniques ▶

For shaping   p. 20

SLEEVES

Using smaller needles and yarn B, cast on
49[51,53,55] sts.
Work in garter st for 8 rows, ending with a
WS row.

Break off yarn B and join in yarn A.
Change to larger needles.
Beg with a k row, work in St st in stripe
sequence as given in box above, shaping

sides by inc one st at each end of 3rd and
every foll 8th[6th,6th,6th] row to 69[61,79,
97] sts, then on every foll 10th[8th,8th,
6th] row until there are 73[81,89,101] sts.
Cont without shaping until sleeve
measures 16½[18,19,20½]in (43[46,49,
52]cm), ending with a WS row.
Bind off.

NECKBAND

Join right shoulder seam.
With RS facing, and using smaller
needles and yarn B, pick up and knit
12[121214] sts down left side of neck,
25[27,29,29] sts from front, 12[12,12,14]
sts up right side of neck, then 35[37,
39,41] sts from back. 84[88,92,98] sts.
Work in garter st for 8 rows.
Bind off knitwise (on WS of work).

TO FINISH

Pin out pieces to figures given in diagram
on the right. Press according to directions
on yarn label.
Join left shoulder and neckband seams.
Set in sleeves. Join side and sleeve
seams.

MEASUREMENTS

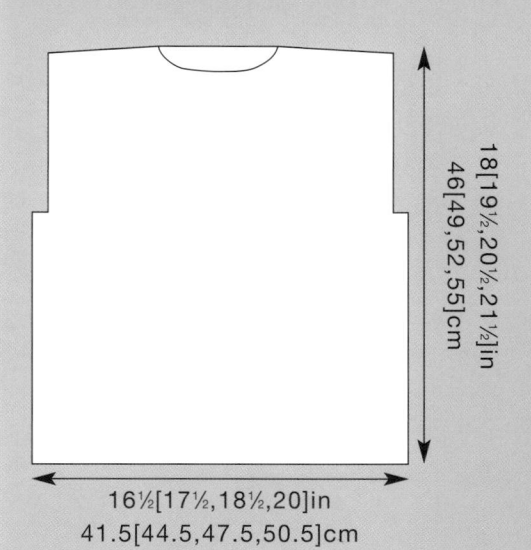

18[19½,20½,21½]in
46[49,52,55]cm

16½[17½,18½,20]in
41.5[44.5,47.5,50.5]cm

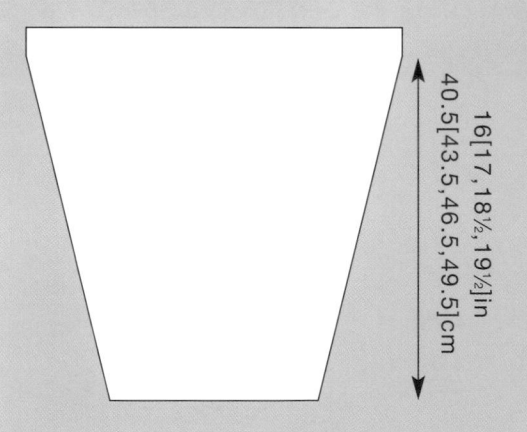

16[17,18½,19½]in
40.5[43.5,46.5,49.5]cm

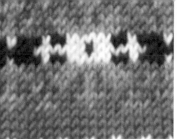

THESE VESTS, WITH
BANDS OF TYPICAL
FAIR ISLE PATTERNS,
MAKE PERFECT
PARTNERS FOR A
COUNTRY WALK, OR
JUST KEEPING WARM
AROUND THE HOUSE.
KNITTED IN A PURE
WOOL ARAN YARN,
THESE GARMENTS
ARE GUARANTEED TO
BE FIRM FAMILY
FAVORITES.

his 'n' hers fair isle vests

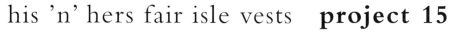

his 'n' hers fair isle vests   **project 15**

his 'n' hers fair isle vests

Both of these vests are knitted in the same four colors, but in variations.
It is interesting to see how rearranging the colors can alter the pattern.
Knit some practice swatches first to see which colorway you prefer.

MEASUREMENTS

To fit Bust/Chest

in	32-34	36-38	40-42	44-46
cm	81- 86	92-97	102-107	112-117

Actual Size

in	36	40	43	47
cm	92	102	110	120

Length

in	20½	22	23½	24¾
cm	52	56	59	63

Figures in brackets [ ] refer to larger sizes;
one set of figures only applies to all sizes.

YOU WILL NEED

Number of 1¾oz (50g) skeins Jaeger
Matchmaker Merino Aran:

Main color (M—755 for hers, 730 for his)

6	6	7	7

A (784)

2	2	2	2

B (730 for hers, 755 for his)

1	1	1	1

C (662)

1	2	2	2

Pair of size 6 (4mm) knitting needles
Pair of size 8 (5mm) knitting needles
Size 6 (4mm) circular knitting needle
5 buttons

GAUGE

20 sts and 22 rows to 4in (10cm) over
patttern on size 8 (5mm) needles or the
size required to give the correct gauge.

ABBREVIATIONS

See page 95.

FAIR ISLE CHART KEY

	Hers	His
○ = M	(755)	(730)
● = A	(784)	(784)
╱ = B	(730)	(755)
☐ = C	(662)	(662)

FAIR ISLE CHART

BACK

Using smaller needles and M, cast on 91[101,109,119] sts.

1st Rib Row: (RS) P1, (k1 tbl, p1) to end.
2nd Rib Row: K1, (p1 tbl, k1) to end.
Rep these 2 rows 3 times more.

Change to larger needles.
Beg with a k row, cont in St st and pat from chart, reading odd-numbered (k) rows from right to left and even-numbered (p) rows from left to right and stranding color not in use loosely across WS of work. Cont in pat until 22 rows have been completed.

These 22 rows form pat. Rep them once more, then work first–8th[12th,16th,20th] rows again.

SHAPE ARMHOLES

Keeping pat correct, bind off 5[6,7,8] sts at beg of next 2 rows. Dec 1 st at each end of next and every foll alt row until 67[71,75,79] sts rem. Cont even until 14th[22nd,8th,16th] row of 5th[5th,6th, 6th] repeat of pat is complete.

SHAPE BACK NECK

Next Row: (RS) Pat 24[25,26,27] sts, turn and complete this side of neck first.
Dec 1 st at neck edge on next 5 rows. Cut off yarn. Leave rem 19[20,21,22] sts on a spare needle.
With RS facing, slip center 19[21,23, 25] sts on to a holder, rejoin yarn to next st and pat to end.
Complete as given for first side of neck.

LEFT FRONT

Using smaller needles and M, cast on 45[49,53,59] sts.
Work 8 rows in rib as given for Back, dec 1 st at end of last row for first and 4th sizes only. 44[49,53,58] sts.

Change to larger needles. Beg with a k row, cont in St st and pat from chart until Front matches Back to armhole, ending with a WS row (for Right Front, end with a RS row here).
1st Row: (RS) Bind off 5[6,7,8] sts, pat to last 2 sts, work 2 tog.

SHAPE ARMHOLE & NECK

Dec 1 st at armhole edge on every foll alt row 7[9,10,12] times in all and AT THE SAME TIME dec one st at front edge on every foll 3rd row. 27[27,29,29] sts. Keeping armhole edge straight, cont to dec at front edge as before until 19[20, 21,22]sts rem.

Cont without shaping until Front matches Back to shoulder. Cut off yarn. Leave sts on a spare needle.

RIGHT FRONT

Work as given for Left Front, noting the bracketed exception.

ARMBANDS

Join right shoulder seam as follows:
With RS tog and back facing, using
larger needles and matching shade,
bind off tog knitwise the 19[20,21,22]
sts of right front with 19[20,21,22] sts
of right back, taking 1 st from each
needle tog each time.

Using smaller needles and M, and with RS
of work facing, pick up and knit 52[55,59,
63] sts around right back armhole, 1 st
from seam, and 52[55,59,63] sts around
right front armhole. 105[111,119,127] sts.
Beg with a 2nd row, work 8 rows in rib as
given for Back. Bind off loosely in rib.
Work left shoulder seam and armband
to match.

FRONT BAND

Using circular needle and M, and with RS
of work facing, pick up and knit 54[57,61,
65] sts along straight edge of right front,
48[52,55,59] sts up right front shaping to
shoulder, 5 sts down right back neck, knit
across 19[21,23,25] back neck sts on
holder, pick up and knit 5 sts up left back
neck, 48[52,55,59] sts down left front
shaping, and 54[57,61,65] sts along
straight edge of left front. 233[249,265,
283] sts.
  Beg with a 2nd row, work 3 rows in rib
as given for Back.

Woman's Version
1st Buttonhole Row: (RS) Rib 4[3,3,3], bind
off next 2 sts, (rib 10[11,12,13] including
st used to bind off, bind off next 2 sts)
4 times, rib to end.

Man's Version
1st Buttonhole Row: (RS) Rib to last 54[57,
61,65] sts, bind off next 2 sts, (rib 10[11,
12,13] including st used to bind off, bind
off next 2 sts) 4 times, rib to end.

Both Versions
2nd Buttonhole Row: Rib to end, casting
on 2 sts over those bound off in previous
row.
Rib 3 rows more. Bind off in rib.

MEASUREMENTS

20½[22,23½,24¾]in
52[56,59,63]cm

18[20,21½,23½]in
46[51,55,60]cm

TO FINISH

Pin out pieces to measurements above.
Press following directions on yarn label.
Join side and armband seams.
Sew on buttons.

techniques

For circular needles p. 26

For buttonholes   p. 43

baby's patchwork blanket

SKILL

2

PRACTICE
MAKES
PERFECT

COVER BABY'S CRIB
WITH A FABULOUS
PATCHWORK BLANKET
WORKED ENTIRELY IN
EASY GARTER STITCH.
AN UNUSUAL
COMBINATION OF
COTTON YARN IN
DUSKY PASTEL SHADES
LOOKS LOVELY IN
THE NURSERY OR
WHEN TAKING YOUR
BABY OUT.

baby's patchwork blanket **project 16**

baby's patchwork blanket

Usually patches are knitted separately and sewn together afterward.
Instead, the seven blocks across a horizontal row here are worked in
sequence with different skeins of yarn, using the intarsia technique.

MEASUREMENTS

Finished blanket is approximately
22½in (57cm) by 28½in (72cm)

YOU WILL NEED

Rowan Wool Cotton—1¾oz (50g) skeins:
1 each of A (shade 900), B (shade 914),
C (shade 929), D (shade 930),
E (shade 942), F (shade 902), and
G (shade 933)

Pair of size 5 (3¾mm) knitting needles

GAUGE

22 sts and 40 rows to 4in (10cm) over
garter st on size 5 (3¾mm) needles or the
size required to give the correct gauge.

ABBREVIATIONS

See page 95.

BLOCK PATTERN DIAGRAM

D	B	G	F	E	C	A
E	F	A	C	A	D	G
C	G	E	D	G	F	B
A	D	F	A	B	E	C
F	B	C	E	D	G	A
D	A	G	B	F	C	E
G	C	D	A	E	B	F
B	A	E	F	G	A	D
F	G	C	A	D	E	B

BLANKET

Using size 5 (3¾mm) needles, cast on as
follows:
18 sts using color F, 18 sts using color G,
18 sts using color C, 18 sts using color A,
18 sts using color D, 18 sts using

color E, and 18 sts using color B. 126 sts.
1st Row: (RS) Knit 18B, 18E, 18D, 18A,
18C, 18G, 18F.

Keeping colors correct as set and
twisting yarns tog when changing colors
to avoid a hole, work in garter st for
31 rows more, ending with a WS row.
First band of blocks completed—each
block should be 3in (8cm) square.
33rd Row: (RS) Knit 18D, 18A, 18G, 18F,
18E, 18A, 18B.
Keeping colors correct as set, work in
garter st for 31 rows more, ending with a
WS row.

Second band of blocks completed.
65th Row: (RS) Knit 18F, 18B, 18E, 18A,
18D, 18C, 18G.
The last row sets position of third band of
blocks.

Cont as now set foll diagram, working
each block as 18 sts and 32 rows of
garter st and using colors as shown on
diagram. When all 9 bands of blocks are
complete, bind off.

TO FINISH

Pin out blanket to the finished
measurement. Cover with damp cloths
and allow to dry. See yarn label for
washing and care instructions.

techniques ▶

For garter stitch   p. 17
For intarsia   p. 31

teddy bear toy

SKILL

(1)

FOR THE
BEGINNER

OUR CUTE TEDDY
BEAR IS SO
CHARMING THAT
YOU'LL WANT TO KNIT
ONE FOR EVERY
CHILD YOU KNOW—AS
WELL AS ONE FOR
YOURSELF. HIS THICK
TWEED "COAT" GIVES
HIM A TRADITIONAL
FLARE.

teddy bear toy   **project 17**

teddy bear toy

Teddy isn't difficult to knit, but he is constructed as a toy so it's important that you follow the finishing instructions carefully to give him neat seams and well-filled proportions.

MEASUREMENTS

Finished teddy is approximately 19in (48cm) tall

YOU WILL NEED

Number of 3½oz (100g) skeins Sirdar Cossack Chunky: 2 skeins (shade 084)

Pair of size 10½ (6½mm) knitting needles
Washable polyester toy stuffing
2 buttons
Wool embroidery yarn in black
28in (70cm) strong cotton tape

GAUGE

12½ sts and 18 rows to 4in (10cm) over St st on size 10½ (6½mm) needles or the size required to give the correct gauge.

ABBREVIATIONS

See page 95.

ssp = Slip the first st, then the 2nd st knitwise, return sts to left needle, take right needle behind to insert it into 2nd, then first st and p2tog.

HEAD

LEFT SIDE

Cast on 12 sts. Beg with a k row, work 4 rows St st.
5th Row: (RS) Inc in first st, k to end. 13 sts. Purl 1 row.
7th Row: Inc in first st, k to last 2 sts, inc in next st, k1. 15 sts.
8th Row: Inc in first st, p to end. 16 sts.
9th and 10th Rows: As 7th and 8th rows. 19 sts.
11th Row: K to last 2 sts, inc in next st,

k1. 20 sts.
12th Row: As 8th row. 21 sts.
13th Row: As 11th row. 22 sts. Purl 1 row.
15th Row: As 11th row. 23 sts. Work 9 rows in St st.**
25th Row: (RS) K1, k2tog, k to end. 22 sts.
26th Row: Bind off 8 sts, p to end. 14 sts.
27th Row: As 25th row. 13 sts. Purl 1 row.
29th Row: K1, k2tog, k to last 3 sts, sl1-k1-psso, k1. 11 sts. Purl 1 row.
31st Row: As 29th row. 9 sts. Purl 1 row. Bind off.

RIGHT SIDE

Reversing shapings, work to match left side to **.
25th Row: (RS) Bind off 8 sts, k to last 3 sts, sl1-k1-psso, k1. 14 sts. Purl 1 row.
27th Row: K to last 3 sts, sl1-k1-psso, k1. 13 sts. Complete as left side.

GUSSET

Cast on 2 sts.
1st Row: (RS) (Inc in next st) twice. 4 sts. Purl 1 row.
3rd Row: (Inc in next st, k1) twice. 6 sts. Work 9 rows in St st.
Inc Row: (RS) Inc in first st, k to last 2 sts, inc in next st, k1. 8 sts.

Inc in this way at each end of next 3 RS rows. 14 sts. Work 25 rows in St st.
Dec Row: K1, k2tog, k to last 3 sts, sl1-k1-psso, k1. 12 sts.
Dec in this way at each end of 2 foll 4th rows and next 2 RS rows. 4 sts.
Work 3 rows in St st. Bind off.

EARS (MAKE 2)

Cast on 18 sts. Beg with a k row, work 4 rows in St st.
Next Row: (RS) K1, (k2tog, sl1-k1-psso) 4 times, k1. 10 sts. Purl 1 row.
Next Row: (RS) K1, k2tog twice, (sl1-k1-psso) twice, k1. 6 sts.
Arrange 3 sts on each needle and graft sts together.

BODY

LEFT HALF

Cast on 13 sts.
1st Row: Inc in first st, k to last 2 sts, inc in next st, k1.
2nd Row: Inc in first st, p to last 2 sts, inc in next st, p1.
Inc in this way at each end of next 3 rows. 23 sts. Purl 1 row. Inc as before at end of next 3 RS rows. 26 sts.
Work 13 rows in St st.
Dec Row: (RS) K1, k2tog, k to last 3 sts, sl1-k1-psso, k1. 24 sts.
Dec in this way at each end of 2 foll 4th rows and next 2 RS rows. 16 sts.
Now dec 1 st at end of next 3 RS rows. 13 sts. Purl 1 row. Bind off.

RIGHT HALF

Reversing all shapings, work to match left half.

LEGS

LEFT OUTER LEG

Cast on 16 sts. Beg with a k row, work 6 rows in St st.
7th Row: (RS) K to last 3 sts, sl1-k1-psso, k1.
8th Row P1, ssp, p to end.
9th, 10th, and 11th Rows: As 7th, 8th, and

7th rows. 11 sts. Purl 1 row.
13th Row: (RS) K1, k2tog, k to last 2 sts, inc in next st, k1.
Work last 2 rows 3 more times. Purl 1 row.
Inc Row: (RS) Inc in first st, k to last 2 sts, inc in next st, k1. 13 sts.
Inc in this way at each end of 2 foll RS rows. 17 sts.
Work 9 rows in St st.
Dec Row: (RS) K1, k2tog, k to last 3 sts, sl1-k1-psso, k1.
Dec in this way at each end of next 3 RS rows.
Last Row: (WS) P1, ssp, p to last 3 sts, p2tog, p1. 7 sts. Bind off.

RIGHT INNER LEG

Work as given for left outer leg.

LEFT INNER LEG

Reversing all shapings, work to match left outer leg.

RIGHT OUTER LEG

As left inner leg.

SOLES (MAKE 2)

Cast on 5 sts. Work in St st, inc 1 st as before at each end of first and 2nd rows. 9 sts. Work 9 rows in St st. Dec one st as before at each end of next 2 rows. 5 sts. Bind off.

ARMS

LEFT OUTER ARM

Cast on 3 sts. Work in St st. (Inc 1 st at each end of next row and 1 st at beg of foll row) twice. 9 sts. Inc 1 st at beg of next and foll RS row. 11 sts. Purl 1 row.
Next Row: (RS) Inc in first st, k to last 3 sts, sl1-k1-psso, k1.
Work last 2 rows 3 times more. Work 3 rows in St st.
Inc 1 st as before at each end of next row. 13 sts.
Purl 1 row.
Next Row: (RS) K1, k2tog, k to last 2 sts, inc in next st, k1.
Work last 2 rows twice more. Work 5 rows

in St st.
Dec as before at each end of next 4 rows. 5 sts. Bind off.

RIGHT INNER ARM

Work as given for left outer arm.

LEFT INNER ARM

Reversing all shapings, work to match left outer arm.

RIGHT OUTER ARM

As left inner arm.

TO FINISH

Leaving a gap at bound-off edges, join sides of body and inner and outer arms and legs. Set in soles. Stuff arms and legs firmly and close gaps. Stuff lower half of body. Thread a large darning needle with a 16-in (40-cm) length of tape. Pin one end of tape to top back seam. Bring needle out of body at left leg position, take through stitches at top of left inner leg, thread tape through body and out at right leg position, take through stitches at top of right inner leg and back into body. Undo pin, pull tape to close legs to body, and knot tape firmly. Stuff top of body and, using remaining tape, join arms in same way. Complete body stuffing, gather bound-off edges, pull tight, and secure.

Join left and right sides of head at chin, insert cast-on point of gusset at nose and sew sides of head to gusset. Stuff head firmly, filling out nose and neck well. Gather neck edge, pull tight, and secure. Sew head onto body, tilting at an angle. Using black thread, embroider nose and mouth as shown in the picture. Use black thread to sew through holes in one button, leaving long ends. Thread a sharp darning needle with one end, place button in left eye position and sew on, taking each end diagonally through head and out slightly apart at right ear position. Pull ends to pull button into head, knot and darn in. Sew on right eye button as before. Sew on ears.

techniques ▶
For grafting stitches p. 42

girl's
crop top

girl's crop top   **project 18**

SKILL

2

PRACTICE
MAKES
PERFECT

GREET THE SUN WITH
THIS FUN TOP IN A
CROPPED STYLE
THAT'S ALL THE RAGE
FOR YOUNGSTERS.
KNITTED IN A COOL
BOUCLÉ YARN AND
BRIGHT, ZINGY
COLORS, IT
FEATURES BOLD
EMBROIDERED DAISY
MOTIFS.

girl's crop top   **project 18**

girl's crop top

Mainly knitted in simple stockinette stitch, the blocks of color around this top's hem are the perfect opportunity for you to try the intarsia technique. You can leave the blocks plain, or decorate them with embroidery.

MEASUREMENTS

To fit Chest							
	in	22	24	26	28	30	32
	cm	56	61	66	71	76	81
Actual Size	in	22	24	26	28	30	32
	cm	56	61	66	71	76	81
Length	in	10¼	11¾	12½	14½	16½	17¾
	cm	26	30	32	37	42	45

Figures in brackets [ ] refer to larger sizes; where there is only one set of figures, it applies to all sizes.

YOU WILL NEED

Number of 1¾oz (50g) skeins Sirdar Tango DK:

A (shade 153)	1	2	2	2	3	3
B (shade 154)	1	1	1	1	1	1
C (shade 152)	1	1	1	1	1	1

Small amount of shade 151 for embroidery

Pair of size 6 (4mm) knitting needles
Pair of size 3 (3¼mm) knitting needles

GAUGE

22sts and 28 rows to 4in (10cm) over St st on size 6 (4mm) needles or the size required to give the correct gauge.

ABBREVIATIONS

See page 95.

BACK & FRONT (ALIKE)

Using smaller needles and A, cast on 60[66,72,78,82,88] sts.
1st and 2nd Rows: Knit.

color knitting

Work the color blocks around the hem of this top, using a separate, small ball of yarn for each block. When changing color, always twist the new color around the color just used to link them together and avoid holes.

3rd and 4th Rows: K1[0,0,2,0,0]A, 2[2,1,2,2,1]B, 2A,*2B, 2A, rep from * to last 3[2,1,4,2,1] sts, 2[2,1,2,2,1]B, 1[0,0,2,0,0]A.
5th–7th Rows: Using A, knit.
8th Row: Using A, knit to end, inc 1 st in center of row. 61[67,73,79,83,89] sts. Change to larger needles and proceed as follows:
1st Row: Using A, knit.
2nd Row: Using A, purl.
These 2 rows will now be referred to as St st (stockinette stitch).
Work 2[2,4,4,6,6] rows more in St st. Proceed as follows:
1st Row: K2[4,5,7,3,3]A, 17B, (3[4, 6,7,3,5]A, 17B) 2[2,2,2,3,3] times, k2 [4,5,7,3,3]A.
2nd Row: P2[4,5,7,3,3]A, k17B, (p3[4,6,7, 3, 5]A, k17B) 2[2,2,2,3,3] times, p2[4,5,7, 3,3]A.
3rd and 4th Rows: As first and 2nd rows.

5th Row: K2[4,5,7,3,3]A, 2B, 13C, 2B, (3[4,6,7,3,5]A, 2B, 13C, 2B) 2[2,2,2,3,3] times, 2[4,5,7,3,3]A.

6th Row: P2[4,5,7,3,3]A, k2B, p13C, k2B, (p3 [4,6,7,3,5]A, k2B, p13C, k2B) 2[2,2,2,3,3] times, p2[4,5,7,3,3]A.

7th–2nd Rows: Rep 5th and 6th rows 8 times more.

23rd–26th Rows: Rep first and 2nd rows twice.

Using A only, cont in St st until work measures 4½[5½,6,7½,9,9½]in (12[14,15, 19,23,25]cm), ending with a WS row.

SHAPE ARMHOLES

Bind off 3 sts at beg of next 2 rows. 55[61,67,73,77,83] sts.

Work 8[10,12,14,14,18] rows, dec 1 st at each end of every row. 39[41,43,45,49,47] sts.

For 5th and 6th sizes only

Work [4,2] rows, dec 1 st at each end of next and foll alt row. [45,45] sts.

SHAPE NECK

For all 6 sizes

Next Row: K2tog, k7[8,8,9,7,7], turn and leave rem 30[31,33,34,36,36] sts on a stitch holder.

Working on these 8[9,9,10,8,8] sts only, proceed as follows,

Next Row: Purl to last 0[2,2,2,0,0] sts, (p2tog) 0[1,1,1,0,0] times. 8[8,8,9,8,8] sts.

For 4th size only

Work 3 rows, dec 1 st at each end of every row. [3] sts.

For 1st, 2nd, 3rd, 5th and 6th sizes only

Work 3 rows, dec 1 st at armhole edge in next and foll alt row and AT THE SAME TIME dec one st at neck edge in every row. 3 sts.

neat borders

To ensure that you pick up stitches evenly around an edge, mark its center and quarter points with pins. Divide the total number of stitches by four, and pick up the same number in each section.

For all 6 sizes

Next Row: Purl.

Next Row: K2tog, k1. 2 sts.

Next Row: P2tog. Fasten off.

With RS facing, working on rem 30[31,33, 34,36,36] sts, slip 21[21,23,23,27,27] sts onto a stitch holder, rejoin yarn to rem 9[10,10,11,9,9] sts and knit to last 2 sts, k2tog.

Next Row: (P2tog) 0[1,1,1,0,0] times, purl to end. 8[8,8,9,8,8] sts.

Complete to match first side of neck, reversing shapings.

ARMHOLE BORDERS

Join side seams.

With RS facing, and using smaller needles and A, pick up and knit 38[42,46,50, 58,62] sts evenly along armhole edge.

1st Row: Knit.

2nd and 3rd Rows: K2A, *2B, 2A, rep from * to end.

4th–6th Rows: Using A, knit.

Bind off knitwise.

techniques ▶

For shaping   p. 20

For intarsia   p. 31

STRAPS & NECKBAND

With RS facing, and using smaller needles and A, cast on 22[22,26,26,26, 26] sts, using same needle and yarn pick up and knit 4 sts evenly along armhole edging, 5 sts evenly along left side of front neck, 21[21,23,23,27,27] sts left on a stitch holder at front of neck, 5 sts evenly along right side of front neck, 4 sts evenly along armhole edging, cast on 22[22,26,26,26,26] sts, 4 sts evenly along armhole edging, 5 sts evenly along right side of back neck, 21[21,23,23, 27,27] sts left on a stitch holder at back of neck, 5 sts evenly along left side of back neck, and 4 sts evenly along armhole edging. 122[122,134,134,142,142] sts.

1st Row: Knit.

2nd and 3rd Rows: K2A, * 2B, 2A, rep from * to end.

4th–6th Rows: Knit.

Bind off knitwise.

TO FINISH

Sew left back of strap in position. Using a scrap of white yarn double, embroider a lazy-daisy-stitch flower in the center of each square. Using B yarn single, embroider bullion stitch in the center of each flower. Pin out garment to the measurements given below. Cover with damp cloths and allow to dry. See yarn label for washing and further care instructions.

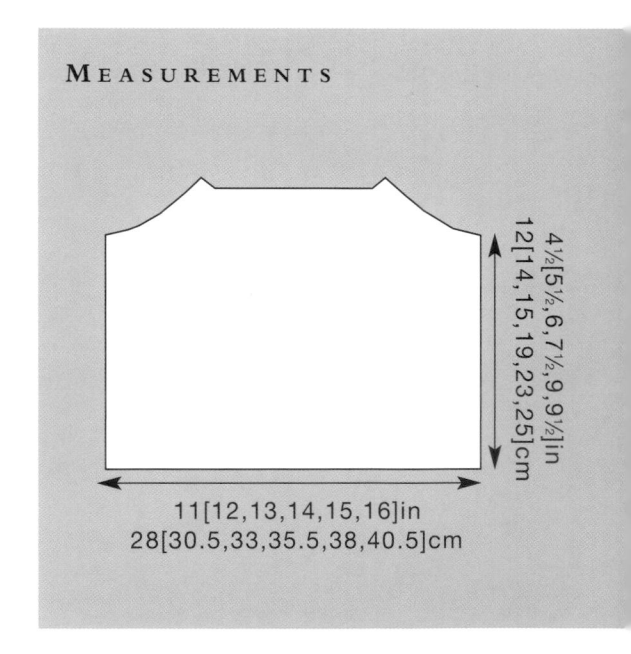

MEASUREMENTS

4½[5½,6,7½,9,9½]in
12[14,15,19,23,25]cm

11[12,13,14,15,16]in
28[30.5,33,35.5,38,40.5]cm

techniques ▶

For lazy daisy stitch p. 39

For finishing off   p. 40

BEAT THE WINTER
BLUES WITH FUNKY,
FASHIONABLE FEET.
THESE KNITTED SOCKS,
WITH BRIGHT FAIR
ISLE DIAMONDS OR
SIMPLE COLORWORK
MOTIFS, ARE WARM
AND SNUGGLY, AND
LOOK GREAT, TOO.

fair isle socks

fair isle socks   **project 19**

fair isle socks

Socks are traditionally knitted on sets of double-pointed needles. The technique might seem complicated at first, but it is easier than it looks and it's great fun to see the pattern taking shape.

MEASUREMENTS

To fit small [medium,large]

Figures in brackets [ ] refer to larger sizes; where there is only one set of figures, it applies to all sizes.

YOU WILL NEED

Diamond-trellis socks
Number of 1¾oz (50g) skeins Sirdar Country Style DK:

A (shade 471)	1	2	2
B (shade 473)	1	1	1
C (shade 489)	1	1	1
D (shade 402)	1	1	1

Fair Isle socks
Number of 1¾oz (50g) skeins Sirdar Country Style DK:

A (shade 478)]	2	2	3
B (shade 473)	1	1	1
C (shade 489)	1	1	1

One set of five size 6 (4mm) double-pointed knitting needles
One set of five size 3 (3¼mm) double-pointed knitting needles

GAUGE

22 sts and 28 rows to 4in (10cm) measured over St st using size 6 (4mm) needles.
26 sts and 26 rows to 4in (10cm) measured over Fair Isle pattern using size 6 (4mm) needles.

start here

To mark the beginning and end of rounds, tie a loop of contrast-colored yarn around the end of the fourth needle. Each time you reach the loop, simply slip it from one needle to the next.

ABBREVIATIONS

See page 95.

DIAMOND-TRELLIS SOCKS

Using a set of smaller double-pointed needles and A, cast on 40[50,60] sts and divide sts on four needles as foll:

10[12,15] sts on needles 1 and 4 and 10[13,15] sts on needles 2 and 3. Join, taking care not to twist sts on needles. Place a marker between needles 1 and 4 to mark beg of round and center back of sock. Work in k1, p1 rib for 2½in (6cm). Change to larger double-pointed needles. Cont in St st and pat from chart. Rep the 20 pat rounds 2[3,3] times, taking care not to pull yarn too tightly across back of work. Cut off yarn.

DIAMOND-TRELLIS CHART

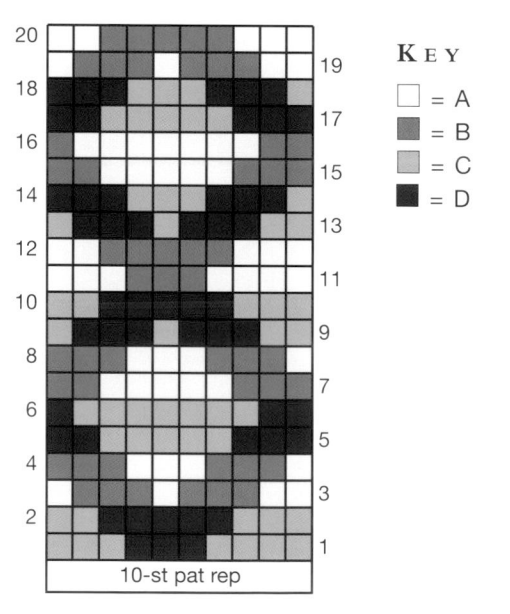

KEY
☐ = A
▨ = B
▨ = C
■ = D

10-st pat rep

techniques ▶

For fair isle and stranding

p. 32-33

HEEL

Using smaller set of double-pointed needles to end, working 20[24,30] sts on needles 1 and 4 only and leaving rem 20[26,30] sts on needles 2 and 3. Using D, work back and forth in St st for 16[20,22] rows.

TURN HEEL

Next Row: (RS) K12[15,19], sl1-k1-psso. Turn work.
Next Row: (WS) Sl1, p4[6,8], sl1-p1-psso. Turn work.
Next Row: Sl1, k4[6,8], sl1-k1-psso. Turn work.
Rep last 2 rows until all sts have been worked from these needles. Cut off yarn. Leave these 6[8,10] sts on needle.

With RS facing and A, pick up and knit 11[13,15] sts along heel edge, knit across 6[8,10] sts from needle, then pick up and knit 11[13,15] sts along other side of heel. 28[34,40] sts. Divide these sts between 2 needles (needles 1 and 4), then work over sts on 2nd, 3rd, and 4th needles to end at center sole. 48[60,70] sts.

GUSSET

Working in St st over all sts, work 1 round.
Dec Round: On needle 1, k to last st, k this st tog with first st on 2nd needle, k to last st on 3rd needle, sl1 then k first st from 4th needle, psso, knit to end. Rep dec round 4 times more. 38[50, 60] sts.Cont even in pat to required length, less about 1¼[1½,2]in (3[4,5]cm) for shaping toe. Cut off yarn.

SHAPE TOE

Join in D and work 2 rounds.
Next Round: On needle 1, k to last 3 sts, k2tog, k1; on needle 2, k1, sl1-k1-psso, k to end; work sts on needle 3 same as needle 1; work sts on needle 4 same as needle 2.
Rep last round until 6[6,8] sts rem. Cut off yarn, leaving a long end. Draw a double strand of yarn through rem sts and fasten off securely.

FAIR ISLE SOCKS

Using a set of smaller double-pointed needles and B, cast on 36[48,60] sts. Divide the sts with 9[12,15] sts on each needle. Join, taking care not to twist

techniques ▶

For using sets of
needles   p. 27

Fair Isle chart

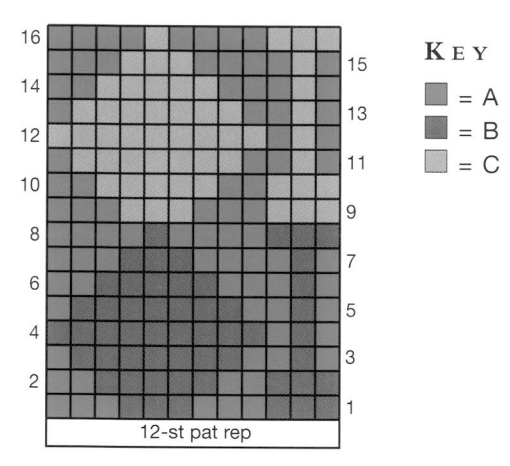

16
15
14
13
12
11
10
9
8
7
6
5
4
3
2
1

12-st pat rep

Key

■ = A
■ = B
■ = C

sts on needles. Place a marker between needles 1 and 4 to mark beg of round and the center back of sock. Working in k1, p1 rib, work 2 rounds. Join in A and cont in rib until work measures 2½in (6cm) from beg. Change to larger double-pointed needles. Cont in St st and pat from chart. Rep the 16 pat rounds 2[3,3] times, then work first–8th rounds again, taking care not to pull yarn too tightly across back of work. Cut off yarn.

Heel

Using smaller set of double-pointed needles to end, work sts on needles 1 and 4 only (18[24,30] sts), leaving rem 18[24,30] sts on needles 2 and 3. Using C, work back and forth in St st for 16[20,22] rows.

Turn Heel

Next Row: (RS) K11[15,19], sl1-k1-psso. Turn work.
Next Row: (WS) Sl1, p4[6,8], sl1-p1-psso. Turn work.
Next Row: Sl1, k4[6,8], sl1-k1-psso. Turn work.

Rep the last 2 rows until all sts have been worked from these needles. Cut off yarn. Leave these 6[8,10] sts on needle.
With right side facing and A, pick up and knit 11[13,15] sts along heel edge, knit across 6[8,10] sts from needle, then pick up and knit 11[13,15] sts along other side of heel. 28[34,40] sts. Divide these sts between 2 needles (needles 1 and 4), then work over sts on 2nd, 3rd and 4th needles to end at center sole. 46[58,70] sts.

Gusset

Cont in St st over all sts, work 1 round.
Dec Round: On needle 1, k to last st, k this st tog with first st on 2nd needle, k to last st on 3rd needle, sl1, then k first st from 4th needle, psso, k to end. Rep dec round 4 times more. 36[48,60] sts.
Cont even in St st to required length, less about 1¼[1½,2]in (3[4,5]cm) for shaping toe. Cut off yarn.

Shape Toe

Join in B and work 2 rounds.
Next Round: On needle 1, k to last 3 sts, k2tog, k1; on needle 2, k1, sl1-k1-psso, k to end; work sts on needle 3 same as needle 1; work sts on needle 4 same as needle 2.
Rep last round until 8 sts rem. Cut off yarn, leaving a long end. Draw a double strand through rem sts and fasten off.

techniques ▶
For stranding yarns

abbreviations

The following are the abbreviations most commonly used in knitting patterns. Special abbreviations are given with the patterns.

alt	alternate		**p**	purl
approx	approximately		**pat**	pattern(s), work in pattern
beg	begin(ning)		**psso**	pass slipped stitch over
cm	centimeter(s)		**rem**	remain(s)(ing)
CN	cable needle		**rep**	repeat(s)(ing)
cont	continu(e)(ing)		**RS**	right side
dec	decreas(e)(ing)		**sl**	slip
foll	follow(s)(ing)		**st(s)**	stitch(es)
g	gram(s)		**St st**	stocking stitch
in	inch(es)		**tbl**	through back loop
inc	increas(e)(ing)		**tog**	together
k	knit		**WS**	wrong side
m	meter(s)		**yb**	yarn to back between two needles
m1	make 1 stitch by picking up loop between last and next st and working into the back of this loop		**yd(s)**	yard(s)
			yf	yarn to front between two needles
mm	millimeter(s)		**yo**	yarn over
oz	ounce(s)			

* Repeat instructions after asterisk or between asterisks as many times as instructed.
() Repeat instructions inside parentheses as many times as instructed.